Murder at the Motel

NIGHTMARE ARIZONA
PARANORMAL COZY MYSTERIES

BETH DOLGNER

Murder at the Motel
Nightmare, Arizona Paranormal Cozy Mysteries, Book Four
© 2023 Beth Dolgner

Print ISBN-13: 978-1-958587-14-0

Murder at the Motel is a work of fiction. Names, characters, places, and incidents either are the products of the author's imagination or are used fictitiously. Any resemblance to actual persons, living or dead, businesses, companies, events, or locales is entirely coincidental.

Published by Redglare Press
Cover by Dark Mojo Designs
Print Formatting by The Madd Formatter

https://bethdolgner.com

CHAPTER ONE

I yawned and blinked at Madge. "Sorry, what?"

Before she could answer, I felt something wet against the back of my hand. Without even bothering to look down, I turned my wrist so I could pet Felipe. "Hey, buddy," I mumbled.

When my fingers felt fur instead of leathery chupacabra skin, I glanced down. It hadn't been Felipe's wet little nose I had felt, but a snout. Zach was sitting on his hind legs, looking up at me with wide black eyes. His rust-red fur shone in the light of the overhead chandelier. He huffed out what I thought was supposed to be a greeting.

I retracted my hand. "Zach, I am not going to pet you. That's weird."

Zach cocked his head. I knew he understood every word I was saying. Even in his werewolf form, Zach still retained his full human consciousness. I bent at the waist, so we were nose to nose. "You," I said, "are a human being most of the time, and I am not going to pet you." I paused, then added, "Especially not in your human form, so don't get any ideas."

Zach huffed again, his tongue lolling out. I wasn't sure if he was amused by my joke or trying to look adorable. Well, as adorable as a werewolf could possibly look,

1

anyway. In answer, I crossed my arms and gazed at Zach with one eyebrow raised.

I had never heard a werewolf sigh, but that was exactly what Zach did, before he rose onto all fours and padded away. We were in the entryway of Nightmare Sanctuary Haunted House, and Zach headed in the direction of the dining room, where he probably hoped to find a staff member who was more open to the idea of giving a werewolf a belly rub.

I stifled another yawn as I lazily watched Zach's retreating form, but when Madge spoke again, I returned my attention to her.

"I asked if you enjoyed your evening." Madge tossed her long blonde curls over her shoulder and peered at me. "You look exhausted."

"Because I am. A guest at the motel was shouting up a storm in the middle of the night. Then, another guest began to shout, probably trying to quiet the first man, but it only added to the racket."

Madge smiled, which made her look even more beautiful. I wanted to ask her if she was born that gorgeous, or if she had used some witchcraft on herself to look that way. "Go home, Olivia, and get some sleep. Tomorrow is Saturday, so we'll be busy here. You need your rest!"

I waved languidly. "I will happily take your advice. Good night, Madge."

I turned and made it all the way to the double front doors of the old building, before I heard firm footsteps coming from the direction of Damien's office. My hand shot out, and I yanked on the door handle, but I was too late to make an escape. Damien called my name, and I turned to him reluctantly.

"Can you please come to my office?" Damien said quietly. He was wearing his mirrored sunglasses, which was never a good sign. It meant his emotions were flaring up, and he was trying to hide the telltale sign of his green eyes glowing.

I opened my mouth to protest. I wanted nothing more than to fall into bed and, hopefully, have a peaceful night in my apartment at Cowboy's Corral Motor Lodge. Damien, though, looked tense, and I knew whatever he wanted to discuss shouldn't wait. I nodded curtly and followed him down a hallway to his office.

At first, I didn't realize someone was sitting in one of the two oxblood leather chairs in front of Damien's desk. Vivian was so petite her head didn't rise above the back of the chair, and I only saw her as I moved to sit down, too. "Oh," I said, suddenly understanding what this was about.

Vivian was a psychic medium. I had met her on my first night of work at the Sanctuary, but I usually only saw her in passing. She and her husband, Amos, tended to keep to themselves. During a recent Friday the Thirteenth party, Vivian had explained to me that her psychic senses could overwhelm her sometimes, so she often had to isolate herself from others to "quiet the noise."

"Hi, Olivia. I already told Damien, but he thought you needed to know, too."

The hesitance in Vivian's voice put me on my guard. "Know what?" I asked. I had been in the process of dropping into the other chair, but I remained standing.

Vivian and Damien exchanged a quick glance. "Vivian didn't pick up on much at the mine," Damien said. Earlier in the day, Vivian had visited the old mine owned by his father, Baxter. The mine had been converted into a home, though it clearly hadn't been lived in for decades. We were hoping we might find clues there that could help us learn more about Baxter's disappearance about eight months before.

"So, there weren't any psychic imprints left on the place?" I asked Vivian.

"I sensed a deep feeling of pain," Vivian said. "But, also…" She fell silent and looked at Damien again.

I felt my chest tighten. I didn't know what was coming, but clearly, it wasn't good.

Vivian tugged nervously at the hem of her vintage shirt. With cropped jeans, a white button-down blouse, and her long dark hair pulled up in a red bandanna, she looked like a pinup queen from the nineteen fifties. "Your name was in my head, Olivia. I don't mean I heard a voice speaking to me. It was more like someone directed my thoughts to you."

"Why?" I wasn't sure if I was upset by that news or simply curious. It certainly seemed to make Vivian uncomfortable.

Vivian shook her head. "I don't know."

"It means I was right. There's a link between you and my father." Damien had been standing, and he finally settled into the chair behind the massive oak desk. "Whether it's a psychic link or something magical, I don't know."

"Again, why?" I pressed. "You've been saying that for a long time now, but we still don't know why I would have a connection to a man I've never met."

Damien took off his sunglasses and slid them into the inner pocket of his tailored gray suit jacket. "I don't know, but I think we were right when we speculated that Sonny's Folly Mine is going to help us find my father."

I turned to Vivian. "What about the pain you sensed? Is it coming from Baxter? And if so, is he feeling pain now, wherever he is, or is it old pain?"

Vivian thought for a few moments before she said, "It's old pain, but I don't know who it's coming from. It could even be coming from more than one person. There was some terrible sorrow in that mine, and it left a strong impression. I didn't pick up on any details, though."

"Thank you for doing this for us," I said. It had been Damien's idea to send Vivian to the mine to see what psychic impressions she might pick up on. The mine was warded against ghosts, so we had known she wouldn't encounter any of those to communicate with, but we had hoped she might get other information.

And she had. It just hadn't been the kind of information we were anticipating.

Damien echoed my thanks, and Vivian told us she was happy to help before leaving. When it was just Damien and me in the office, I looked at him and asked, again, "Why me?"

"Maybe because you're a conjuror, and your magic will be the key to finding my father."

At first, I had argued with Damien a lot when he suggested I was a conjuror. I was certain I wasn't supernatural at all. But, as time had gone on, I had realized Damien's insistence about me being able to desire something so much that I could magically make it happen wasn't just him being stubborn.

He wanted it to be true because it gave him hope that we would find Baxter.

So, over the last couple of weeks, I had stopped arguing with Damien about it. Instead, I was willingly letting him give me lessons in controlling my thoughts and emotions to hone my alleged skills. It sometimes took an enormous amount of patience on my part, but it wasn't doing any harm, and it made Damien feel better.

There wasn't much else to say after Vivian had left. We could speculate all night long about what she had sensed in the mine, but it wouldn't get us any closer to knowing the truth. So, I wished Damien a good night and walked to my car as fast as I could. I didn't want anyone else asking for a moment of my time.

When I pulled into the parking lot of Cowboy's Corral

Motor Lodge, I was surprised to find nearly every spot was taken. I had never seen the motel so full before. The parking lot sat between the two cinderblock wings of the motel, which ran perpendicular to the road. At the front of the property, a two-story office building sat right in the middle of the driveways into and out of the parking lot.

My efficiency apartment was at the rear of the wing on the right, but I had to drive past it and loop around as I hunted for a parking spot. I eventually ended up near the office.

As I cut through the parking lot on the way to my apartment, I heard a loud voice and looked over to see a man on a cell phone. He was pacing back and forth in front of a ground-floor room almost directly beneath my own. I recognized the voice as the one I had heard shouting the night before.

This time, the man was yelling into the phone about needing to cancel a contract. "I'm not going to be back, so why would I want to keep paying for it?" he yelled. With his free hand, the man reached up and tugged at his thinning brown hair.

A moment later, he added, "That's the most ridiculous thing I've ever heard!"

You're the most ridiculous thing I've ever heard, I thought. Being tired made me snarky.

A voice boomed from somewhere nearby. "Keep it down, or I'll call the police!" It must have been the same guest who had been yelling at the loud man the night before.

I groaned and trudged up my stairs. Even once I had closed the door of my apartment, I could still hear the shouting. I quickly put on my pajamas, washed my face, and fell into bed. I lay on my side and clamped a pillow over my ear. It turned the shouting into a low drone, and I fell asleep within minutes.

When I woke up on Saturday morning, I stretched and rubbed my eyes. It was bright in my apartment. Too bright.

My front door was standing wide open, the sun shining onto my orange shag rug. In the open doorway, I could see the backlit silhouette of a man.

CHAPTER TWO

I leaped out of bed, and I could hear the way my voice shook with both fear and adrenaline as I shouted, "Who are you?"

The man took a few steps forward, and I instinctively grabbed my comforter, holding a corner of it in front of me like a shield. As if that would keep me safe from an intruder.

Once he was inside and no longer in the glare of the sun, though, I could see the man was wearing jeans and a work shirt that bulged over a beer belly. He had a toolbox in one hand. "Oh, sorry, ma'am," he said in a deep voice. "I had understood the room would be unoccupied at this hour."

"Who are you?" I asked again, though slightly less wildly this time around.

"Sammy Simms, from Simms Plumbing."

I lowered the edge of the comforter slightly. "You're a plumber?"

"Yes. I came to fix your broken shower."

I shook my head. "My shower is fine. I think you got the wrong room."

Sammy glanced back, toward my open front door, where *A2* was painted in a faded gold. "Ohhh... I'm

supposed to be downstairs. My apologies for the inconvenience."

"No problem," I said, though internally, I was still feeling on edge. I could understand that Sammy might have gotten the wrong room, but how he had been able to unlock my door was a mystery. As Sammy walked out, closing the door as he went, I consoled myself with the idea that Mama must have given him a skeleton key that could unlock any of the motel doors.

At the same time, though, I chided myself for not having used the security chain. If I'd put it in place the night before, Sammy would have only been able to open the door about three inches, and I wouldn't have woken up to a complete stranger in my apartment.

It seemed pointless to turn on my coffee maker. After the jolt of adrenaline my unexpected visitor had sent coursing through me, I was already wide awake and humming with energy. Still, out of habit, I hit the button and got the coffee started while I took a quick shower. Of course, I didn't do any of that before engaging the security chain on my door in case someone else tried to wander in.

I had just put conditioner in my shoulder-length auburn hair when the shower sputtered and stopped flowing. I twisted the handles, jiggled the lever that switched the water flow between the bath and the shower, and muttered a few swear words for good measure, but none of it made a difference.

Great, now I do need a plumber.

I wrapped a towel around myself and tried the bathroom sink with no luck. I tried the kitchen sink next, but it was clear my apartment suddenly had no water. There was, however, a pitcher of water in my fridge. I reluctantly pulled it out, held my head over the kitchen sink, and began to pour.

I screeched as the icy water tumbled over my head, but

by the time the pitcher was empty, I had at least rinsed most of the conditioner out of my hair. I towel-dried my hair briskly, trying to warm myself up, then got dressed in jeans and a long-sleeved blue blouse. It was shorts weather outside, but I was too chilled for that option just yet.

Once I had dry hair, I headed to the front office to talk to Mama about the plumber's unexpected visit. The office's thick brown carpet and Formica countertop were as retro-kitsch as my own apartment's decor. Mama's voluminous, wavy gray hair stuck up from behind the counter, and it was moving rhythmically. I could hear an oldies tune playing quietly, and as I got closer, I could see Mama sitting at the computer behind the countertop, her lips moving with the lyrics.

She looked up and smiled, her bright blue eyes shining. "Hi, there, Olivia. How are you this morning?"

"Actually, I've come to report that I have no water. I'm sure it has to do with the plumber who showed up in my apartment this morning."

Mama's eyes narrowed. "The water should be back on in no time, but tell me more about Sammy."

I briefly explained how I had woken up to find Sammy standing in my doorway, and as I talked, Mama's expression turned dark. When I had finished, she said, "I don't like that. I gave him a key to room twelve, and that's the only door that key will open. I don't understand how he was able to unlock your door."

"It's a mystery, if you didn't give him a skeleton key."

"I'll ask him about it," Mama assured me. "Sammy has been our plumber here for a few years now, so maybe I did give him a skeleton key at some point and forgot."

I promised Mama I would get some marketing work done for the motel later that afternoon. After all, I did the work in exchange for free rent on my apartment, and I didn't want her to think I wasn't pulling my weight. First, though, I was going hiking.

I wasn't really the outdoors type, but when my friends and co-workers Justine and Clara had asked me to join them, I decided it would be a good chance to get to know both of them better. Besides, they had promised me it wouldn't be a strenuous hike.

The walk back to my apartment after my chat with Mama finally drove the chill out of my bones. The sunshine was still warm, even though it was the first of October. I changed into a pair of khaki shorts and a white tank top, then made the drive to a recreation area south of Nightmare. Justine had instructed me to meet her and Clara at the parking lot where a trail with the ominous name of Turn Back Trail began.

I parked and walked up to find Clara staring at a map posted on a wooden signboard. She had crammed a black cowboy hat down over her ears to hide their pointed tips, and her dark sunglasses ensured no one would spot her violet-colored eyes. Both features were a dead giveaway that she was a fairy.

"Hi, Clara," I called.

Clara turned in my direction and gave me a big smile. She was dressed in green leggings and a ratty black Nightmare Sanctuary Haunted House T-shirt. "Happy Halloween season, Olivia!" she called in her childlike voice.

I laughed. "I thought Halloween was just one day, not a whole season."

"You haven't experienced October in Nightmare yet! It's the start of the town's tourist season now that the heat is dying down, and half the businesses here suddenly start bragging about every unexplained creak or alleged ghost sighting. The saloon even does séances."

"Wow, I had no idea." At least Clara's news helped

explain why it had been so tough to find a parking spot the night before at the motel. I made a mental note to ask Mama if I could get my very own reserved parking place at the bottom of my stairs.

"Oh, yeah," I heard Justine say behind me. I glanced over my shoulder to see her walking up while carrying a bulging backpack, which she patted. "I forgot to get our lunch out of the trunk."

"If Nightmare is a haven for Halloween fans, then I'm guessing we'll be busier than ever at the Sanctuary," I speculated.

Justine slid her arms into the backpack, then began to wind her long chestnut waves into a knot on the top of her head. "Oh, just wait," she promised. "You'll be over-whelmed by all the guests who come to the haunt."

As the three of us began to walk along the trail, which led through a cluster of scrubby trees, Clara said, "Speaking of guests, did you know we had one show up at eight o'clock this morning? I'm amazed anyone was even awake to answer his knocks at the front door."

"I must have slept through it, but why would anyone show up at a haunted house at that hour?" Justine sounded offended by the very idea of it.

"Madge told me he was there demanding to see what he called 'the psychic.'" Clara shrugged. "I guess he needed to know his fortune and couldn't wait until a decent time."

I wondered if Vivian had been roused from sleep and whether she needed a cup of coffee before feeling awake enough to use her psychic abilities. "I didn't realize she gave readings," I said. "I know she's very perceptive, and that she can communicate with ghosts, but I thought she only worked at the Sanctuary."

Justine had been slightly ahead of me, and she slowed until we were walking next to each other. She gave me a curious look. "Viv makes extra cash doing readings from time to time. She doesn't advertise her services, because she doesn't want to step on the toes of Nightmare's resident psychic, but she gets a few clients through word of mouth."

Justine was still giving me that same look, and I prompted, "Just say whatever it is that's on your mind."

"Well... Speaking of Vivian, is it true she visited that mine Theo stayed in a while back?"

"And is it true that Baxter owns it?" Clara asked eagerly.

"Yes, and yes," I confirmed. "And, before you ask, yes, it really was converted into a house, with bedrooms and everything. Judging by the awful color schemes, I'd say it was done in the late sixties or early seventies."

Clara made a little gagging noise. "Our parents' generation had terrible taste."

"You'll never get to see it for yourself," I said. "It's warded with iron."

Clara stopped walking abruptly, and Justine and I turned to look at her. "It's warded against fairies?" she asked.

"And ghosts. Plus, there are tiny silver spikes in the walls to ward against werewolves."

"That doesn't sound like something Baxter would do." Clara's tone was low, almost pouty.

"Damien and I said the same thing," I agreed.

"I wonder what Baxter was hiding from," Justine said slowly, picking at a button on her plaid shirt, "or what he was hiding from the supernatural community."

"Oh, I hadn't even thought of that second option." I stared at the ground, picturing the mine in my head. Damien and I had thought Baxter was trying to keep himself safe in there, and it never occurred to me that maybe Baxter was trying to keep the supernatural community safe from something—some living thing, probably—that was inside the mine. Despite the warm day, I felt a shiver work its way up my spine.

We started walking again, and we continued to speculate about the mine all the way to the trail's end. The ground had been rising gradually as we walked, and we were rewarded with a spectacular view of the rolling hills for miles around. Mountains in the east stood out darkly against the blue sky.

By the time we were settled onto large rocks to enjoy the sandwiches and chips Justine had packed, we had moved on to other subjects. I spent a fair amount of time complaining about Zach expecting me to pet him when he was in his werewolf form. "It's just weird, you know? I'm not going to scratch his ears when he's human, so why would I do it when he's a werewolf?"

Clara snickered. "At least he's housebroken!"

By the time I got back to the motel that afternoon, I was tired but in a good way. The night before, I had felt weary from a lack of sleep and a busy night at work. After the hike, I was tired in a way that made me feel like I had accomplished something.

I took a shower, grateful to have running water again, then headed to the front office with my laptop. I was updating the motel's social media pages, and I needed some input from Mama.

As soon as I walked through the glass door of the office, I regretted it. The loud man who had been shouting into the phone the night before was standing at the counter, his fingers curled around its edge. "I'm telling you, he's a thief!" The man was yelling at Mama, who was standing with her hands on her hips and a defiant look on her face. "That plumber stole my valuables!"

CHAPTER THREE

"Mr. Evers, perhaps you misplaced your... What did you say is missing?" Mama's voice was overly sweet, like she was hoping to charm the man into calming down.

"Antique jewelry," the man said tightly. "Diamonds, rubies. The collection of generations of the Evers family."

"Where is the last place you saw them?"

"Hidden in my suitcase."

I couldn't see the man's face, but I could tell he was talking through clenched teeth.

"Would you like someone to help you make a search of your room?" Mama asked.

"No, because they're not in my room. That plumber stole them when he was working on my shower."

Mama straightened her shoulders, looking even more defiant. "I've been working with Sammy for the past three years, and not one single guest has ever reported things going missing after he'd done work in their room. I think it's unlikely he has suddenly started a criminal career."

Mr. Evers pounded his fists on the countertop so hard I jumped from surprise. He started yelling again. "I don't care what other guests have said! I'm saying that he stole from me!"

Mama raised her hands and took half a step back. "If

you really believe that, then this is a matter for the police. I suggest you call them and file a report."

"That's why I came up here! You need to call the police right now!"

Mama shook her head adamantly. "No, *you* need to. I will write down their number for you, or you can file your report in person. The police station isn't far from here. Would you like directions?"

Mr. Evers made a noise of disgust, then sneered, "I can find it myself. Thanks for nothing." He whirled around, and I jumped out of his path so I wouldn't get plowed over. His round face was twisted in rage, and as he passed by me, I heard him muttering a lot of unkind words that I'm pretty sure were directed at Mama.

Once the door had closed and we were alone, I asked Mama, "You okay?"

Mama gave herself a little shake. "Yeah. Horrible man."

"I can't imagine anyone is getting sleep as long as he's staying here. He was shouting again in the middle of the night."

"Other guests have said the same thing. I am one more guest complaint away from kicking Leonard Evers out of my motor lodge." Mama took a deep breath and let it out with a sigh.

"What's he doing in Nightmare, anyway?" I asked.

"I'm not sure. He made it sound like he's relocating from Ohio to Arizona, so I assume he's looking for a place to live."

I laughed weakly, letting out the tension I realized I was holding onto after witnessing the exchange between Leonard and Mama. "In that case, I sure hope he finds his dream house soon!"

While I worked from one of the lobby chairs that afternoon, I kept one eye on the screen of my laptop and the other on the front door. If Leonard decided to come back and start shouting some more, I wanted to be ready for it. I also half-expected the police to show up to ask about Leonard's claim he'd been robbed by Sammy.

Instead, the only people who came through the door were a handful of tourists who were checking in for the night.

I was having a hard time shaking off the uncomfortable feeling Leonard had given me during his confrontation with Mama. I didn't like hearing anyone being so aggressive, and it made it worse that it was directed toward one of the sweetest women I had ever met. I decided to walk to work that night in the hope that moving my body would get my brain moving on to a new subject.

After walking down a road that ran west for nearly a mile, I turned right at the old gallows and followed the narrow dirt lane that led to the Sanctuary. The days were getting shorter, and it was nearly dark by the time I crested a gentle hill and caught sight of the former hospital building. The weather-stained gray stonework looked spooky, but a few bright lights were burning in upstairs windows. I knew my co-workers were in their apartments, getting ready for that night's work. Despite the imposing building, the warm lights managed to give the place a welcoming feel. Whatever the Sanctuary might look like on the outside, my friends were inside.

As soon as I walked through the double front doors and into the spacious entryway, I ran into Damien, who was coming from a doorway on the left-hand side that led into the haunt itself. "What happened?" he asked immediately.

I pressed a hand against my face. "Is it really showing that much?"

Damien just nodded, and I briefly told him about the worst motel guest in the history of Cowboy's Corral.

I didn't know how I had expected Damien to react, but

his laughter caught me totally off guard. "How can you laugh?" I asked incredulously. "He was so rude to Mama!"

Damien sobered quickly. "Oh, I'm angry about that, believe me. I laughed because this provides the perfect exercise for you. I can tell how much this Leonard guy bothers you, so your strong desire to have him out of the motel is a great chance for you to practice conjuring. You really should set your heart on him finding that dream house as soon as possible."

"I do wish for him to leave," I agreed. "I truly wish he finds a new home soon. A great waterfront property."

"But that's nowhere around here."

"Exactly!"

Damien laughed again, and I felt pride well up in me that I had managed to make him do that. Damien tended to be the stoic type, and that was on a good day, when he wasn't acting like he had a chip on his shoulder the size of a mountain.

I took Damien's advice to heart. As I sat in the massive dining room and listened to Justine make announcements during the family meeting that happened each night before the haunt opened, I focused on how much I wished Leonard Evers would find his new home the very next day and leave Cowboy's Corral behind forever. I was concentrating so hard I nearly missed hearing Justine announce I would be in my usual spot at the front entrance, greeting guests and tearing tickets.

By the time the Sanctuary opened at eight o'clock, there was a line of people snaking back and forth inside the entryway. I could barely see the brass stanchions and red velvet ropes because there were so many people packed inside the dim room. Even the spooky, atmospheric orchestral music that played from hidden speakers could barely be heard over the din of excited guests. Every now and then, someone would emit a shriek, even though there was nothing remotely scary about the entryway.

I was so absorbed in tearing tickets, greeting people, and answering the usual questions—"Where's the bathroom?" and "Just how scary is it?" were the top two—that I entirely forgot about Leonard Evers.

Until he suddenly appeared right in front of me. He elbowed his way past the line of people waiting to get in and began to shove past me, too. I planted my feet in the open doorway and said firmly, "Sir, you have to wait in line, and you need a ticket."

"I have to see her!"

"Her, who?" I asked calmly.

"The psychic, of course! The real one!"

"Mr. Evers, she's working the haunt right now, like the rest of us. I'm sure she'd be happy to give you a reading tomorrow."

Leonard started when I called him by name, and he peered at me. "Are you a psychic, too? Maybe you can help me!"

"I'm not a psychic. I'm your neighbor. I live upstairs from you at Cowboy's Corral." Leonard was standing entirely too close to me, and I was resisting the urge to take a step back. If I did that, he might be able to squirm his way through the door and take off. I knew he must be the person who had shown up at the Sanctuary that morning, demanding to see Vivian, and I wondered if he had acted the same way on that visit.

Leonard leaned even closer, squinting. "Oh. Yeah. You."

I began to relax, thinking he was calming down, when he said loudly, "Then you have to let me through! You know what happened to me with that plumber, but that's not the half of it! I have to see the psychic! I need help!"

The people at the front of the line had fallen silent,

and they were watching the exchange with a mixture of amusement and horror. Leonard's distress was frightening, and I suddenly worried he was going to get violent if I didn't relent and let him in. Still, though, it seemed safer for me to hold him at bay than to let him anywhere near Vivian. It was like he was obsessed with seeing her.

I felt a hand on my shoulder. "Olivia, is this man giving you trouble?" I turned and saw Malcolm towering behind me. His dark eyes glittered in his pale, gaunt face.

I gestured toward Leonard. "He insists on seeing Vivian, but I've told him she's working."

"Whatever she's doing," Leonard said wildly, "it's not as important as helping me!"

"Sir," Malcolm said smoothly, "I'm sure Vivian will be happy to set an appointment with you in the near future. In the meantime, only guests with a ticket can come inside."

That was the wrong thing to say. Leonard's face lit up. "I'll buy a ticket! I'll buy a ticket and find her inside the haunted house!"

Malcolm deftly slid past me and put a bony hand out to stop Leonard from rushing toward the ticket window, where Clara was covering for Zach until the full moon began to wane. "No, sir, I'm afraid you need to leave."

Malcolm swept off his tall black top hat and handed it to me wordlessly. In one deft movement, he slid a hand around Leonard's upper arm and pivoted him in the direction of the parking lot. Leonard tried to squirm out of Malcolm's grip, but it was to no avail. I still didn't know what kind of supernatural creature Malcolm was, but he was impressively strong for such a scrawny man.

Just before Malcolm escorted Leonard outside the glow of lights at the entrance to the Sanctuary, Leonard twisted around and glared at me. "You're making a mistake!" he shouted. "If I die tonight, it's your fault!"

CHAPTER FOUR

I stared toward the parking lot long after Malcolm and Leonard had disappeared into the darkness. My fingers curled around the brim of Malcolm's top hat, and I hoped fervently he would be safe. Leonard seemed more than hysterical. He seemed dangerous.

Finally, reluctantly, I returned my attention to the people standing just in front of me, patiently waiting to have their tickets taken so they could join the queue inside. "My apologies for the interruption," I said, forcing a pleasant smile onto my face. "Please, come in."

"Are you kidding?" said a woman who was bouncing up and down in excitement. "That was amazing! I thought maybe that guy was an actor, and you staged everything to make us more scared!"

"No, unfortunately, it wasn't staged," I said as I reached out for her ticket.

"Is it true?" asked another woman. "Is there a real psychic here?"

"You'll have to decide for yourself when you see her," I said coyly. The fact the Sanctuary was populated by real supernatural creatures was a closely guarded secret, and I didn't want to give away anything about Vivian that might make guests wonder about the rest of the staff.

The next ten people all made some comment to me as

they passed by, excited by the drama they had just witnessed. I realized at some point that my hands were shaking, and I took a few deep breaths in an effort to calm down.

It wasn't until Malcolm returned that I felt like my heart rate finally slowed down to its normal pace. He was dusting off his long black coat as he walked up to me. "Everything good?" I asked.

"I watched your friend drive away, and I'll be sticking close to you for the rest of the night in case he doubles back." Unlike me, Malcolm seemed completely unruffled by the whole thing.

I thanked Malcolm at least three times as I handed back his top hat, promising I would fill him in after work with all the details about what had transpired with Leonard earlier in the day and his antics at the motel. "And," I added, "we need to let Vivian know about this."

There was still an hour left before the Sanctuary closed for the night, and I felt like I spent every second of it on high alert. The crowds began to thin at eleven thirty, and by the time the last group of guests trickled through at ten minutes to midnight, I was exhausted. I slumped against the doorframe and sighed. "Finally," I breathed.

Malcolm and I shut and locked the doors, then split up. I headed down one of the hallways in the east wing toward the dining room while Malcolm made a beeline for the vignette inside the haunt where Vivian was usually stationed.

The dining room had long wooden tables arranged in rows, with benches instead of chairs. Instead of sitting, I lay down on a bench and threw an arm over my face to block the glare of the overhead lights. When something wet touched my elbow, I said, "That had better be you, Felipe."

There was no answer, of course, so I lifted my arm and

turned to see the chupacabra looking at me expectantly. His little white fangs stood out against his leathery gray skin. "I'll pet *you* anytime," I said, reaching out to scratch his head. "Just don't tell Zach, okay? He might get jealous."

Felipe's owner, Mori, came up as I reluctantly moved into a seated position. She sat down gracefully on the bench next to me. She moved regally, and I remembered she had been introduced to me as Countess Moreau. She certainly had a royal air, with her long blood-red gown and her black hair pulled up in a high coiffure. Mori was one of those women—well, vampires—who didn't need makeup to look beautiful, but on this night, she was wearing shimmery golden eyeshadow that really popped against her dark skin. The eyeshadow, I realized, was the exact same shade as her eyes.

"I hear you had quite the adventure tonight," Mori said conversationally.

"Yeah. I'm waiting for Vivian to get here, and then I'll spill all the details for anyone who wants to hear them." Even as I was saying that, Vivian came rushing through the dining room door, followed closely by Malcolm. Unfortunately, I saw that Damien was just behind him.

Oh, great.

After my initial disappointment at seeing Damien, since I naturally assumed he would somehow make the whole thing my fault, I felt a sense of relief. Despite his difficult attitude, I also knew Damien had my back. If he was keeping an eye out for me, then I felt safer.

Vivian was still in the costume she wore for playing her role as a fortune teller in the haunted cabin vignette. The room she worked in was made to resemble a creepy abandoned cabin in a swamp, complete with broken windows that looked out onto moonlit trees dripping with Spanish moss. Vivian would sit behind a table with Tarot cards spread out in front of her, and by flicking a hidden switch, the crystal ball sitting on the table would suddenly rise into the air, as if by itself.

The ratty white cotton dress and mountains of costume jewelry Vivian wore helped sell the role, and her many bangle bracelets jangled as she rushed toward me. "Olivia, what happened? It was that guy Leonard, wasn't it?"

I nodded. "He's a client of yours, apparently?"

Vivian made a scoffing noise and rolled her eyes. "He came to see me this morning, and I refuse to ever sit with him again. He was...odd."

Mori swept an arm around the room. "Considering the company, he must have been *very* odd for you to think that."

I filled Vivian in on Leonard's appearance at the front entrance, then told her everything I knew about him from the motel. She made a face of disgust when I said he was my downstairs neighbor. When I finished, she said, "None of what you're saying surprises me. He was in a similar state when he came to see me. Frantic and deathly afraid, I would say."

"Do you know why?" Malcolm asked.

Vivian hesitated. "I don't usually disclose what I discuss with clients. Sometimes, they talk about really personal things, and I don't want to break their trust, no matter how bizarre I find the person. I will say, though, death was on Leonard's mind when he came to see me this morning, so I'm not surprised he was still thinking of it tonight. He might be a bit delusional, but hopefully, he's harmless."

There wasn't much more to discuss after that, though Malcolm promised he would patrol the grounds that night in case Leonard came back. Mori offered to stay with me, but I assured her I would be fine. After all, Leonard hadn't hurt me, or even threatened me. I figured I was safe.

When I stood up, Vivian gave me a hug. "Thanks for keeping him out. It was the right call."

"I'm a ticket taker *and* a bouncer!" I smiled.

Vivian was already pulling bracelets off her wrist as she left to change out of her costume. Mori said something about going out to find a tourist so she could have some dinner, and Malcolm trailed after her. Soon, it was just me and Damien standing there in the dining room.

I braced myself for Damien to say something critical about how I had handled the situation. I couldn't help it. Even though he had softened up since he had first appeared in Nightmare to take over running the Sanctuary, I still anticipated him being a jerk at every turn.

So I was surprised when he said, "It's bad enough he yelled at Mama, but now he's bringing his drama to the Sanctuary. It's not right for him to make anyone here feel unsafe. Do you want me to stay with you tonight?"

"No," I said quickly. "Like I told Mori, I'll be fine on my own." When Damien just gazed at me wordlessly, I added, "I appreciate the offer, though."

"I was serious when I said earlier that you should treat this situation as a conjuring exercise, but I mean it more than ever now. I want your mind to be fixed on wishing for him to get out of Nightmare by tomorrow."

"Leonard and his dream house will be all I think of from now until I fall asleep. I'll probably dream about him, too."

Damien nodded. "Good."

My promise to Damien wasn't hard to keep, but I was also wishing I wouldn't run into Leonard again when I got back to Cowboy's Corral. Thankfully, I didn't see another soul in the parking lot, and I didn't hear a peep. No one was shouting as I scooted up the stairs and locked myself inside my apartment. This time, I remembered to engage the security chain.

Everything was quiet when I went to bed, but sleep didn't come easily. My brain was still running at full speed, partly from working so hard on my wishing and partly from a lingering fear. Because, no matter how much I told myself I was safe, I still felt vulnerable.

Finally, though, I drifted off. I was in the middle of a dream about walking through the west wing of the Sanctuary, talking about each vignette of the haunted house attraction as if I were a real estate agent showing the place to a potential buyer, when I woke suddenly. I sat up straight in bed.

I had heard something. A loud noise had woken me up. *Right?* I leaned forward slightly, listening. I didn't hear anything, so what had woken me up? In my dream, there had been a loud bang, but I didn't know if the sound had come from the real world or not.

As I sat there, I realized the only noise I could hear was my own breathing. I flopped back onto my pillow and tried to get back to sleep, but it wasn't easy. Even after I did drift off again, I kept waking up, and when I opened my eyes one time to see a faint light coming through my windows, I gave up and got out of bed.

"A night with no shouting, and I still can't get decent rest," I mumbled grumpily as I shuffled to my coffee maker. While it was percolating, I drew aside the curtain in the kitchen window. Judging by the orange and pink hues in the sky, it was just past dawn.

I showered and got dressed, but instead of sitting down to a cup of coffee afterward, I filled up a travel mug to take with me on a leisurely walk. I breathed deeply when I opened my front door, enjoying the slight chill in the air.

When I reached the bottom of the stairs, I turned left, toward the front of the motel, planning to stroll over to High Noon Boulevard to take in the Wild West–style street before the tourists woke up and jammed the boardwalks.

I had taken a few steps before I realized I was walking on a wet sidewalk. My eyes scanned the area ahead of me, and I saw that water was falling over the doorstep of a room.

The door was slightly ajar, and even though my brain was screaming at me not to go any closer, it was like I was compelled to walk up to the door and push it open.

The shag carpet inside was soaked with water, and when I stepped onto it, the water squished up and soaked into my canvas sneakers.

"Hello?" I called.

There was no answer, so I took a few more tentative steps. There were two double beds in the room, and as I reached the space between them, I could see something dark on the floor. As my eyes adjusted to the dim light, I could tell the something was a man.

Leonard was curled up on his side, his eyes wide open and staring into the space underneath one of the beds.

He was dead.

CHAPTER FIVE

I began to back away slowly, as if Leonard was only sleeping, and I might disturb him. I stumbled when my heel hit the threshold, and I went flailing backward out the door, the water on the sidewalk splashing around my feet as I tried to regain my balance.

As soon as I was steady on my feet again, I ran to the front office. Even as I tugged on the glass door, I realized it was far too early for Mama or her husband, Benny, to be there yet. Instead, I set my coffee mug on the bench in front of the office and pulled out my cell phone, then dialed nine-one-one with shaking fingers.

I barely registered my conversation with the dispatcher. I was in shock, and my brain seemed to be running on autopilot. Once the dispatcher promised the police were on their way, I sat down on the bench, feeling dazed.

By the time a Nightmare Police Department car pulled up in front of the office, I was sipping my coffee. I knew the horror of what I had just seen was going to sink in at some point. Until then, I saw no reason to let my coffee go to waste.

It was Officer Reyes who got out of the squad car, and I could see the way his shoulders slumped when he realized it was me sitting there. His stance and the look in his reddish-brown eyes clearly said, *Here we go again.* "You called in a murder?" he asked in a resigned voice.

I nodded. Even as I did, I saw an ambulance shoot past, heading for Leonard's room.

"So you figured you'd enjoy a quiet morning until we turned up?"

I glanced down at my travel mug, then looked at Officer Reyes with a shrug. "I didn't know what else to do." My voice cracked. Talking to Reyes was making the reality of the situation set in.

Reyes seemed to know it, too, because his voice was kinder when he spoke again. "Tell me what happened, Ms. Kendrick."

I briefly explained that I had followed the flood to Leonard's door, then found him inside. When I was done, Reyes said, "And you're sure he was dead?"

"Well, I'm not totally certain, but I'd be willing to bet money on it."

An EMT rounded the corner of the office and walked up to us. He barely glanced at me. "We can't help," he told Reyes in a low voice.

Reyes nodded toward me. "You don't have to use delicate language in front of Ms. Kendrick. She's no stranger to death. The question is, how did he die?"

The EMT's lips compressed into a thin line. He still spoke quietly. "Gunshot to the chest."

Reyes sighed. "He was murdered, then." He looked down at me as he took off his cap and ran a hand through his dark hair. "Ms. Kendrick, I had hoped you were done jumping into the middle of murder investigations."

"I just wanted to take a walk and drink my coffee," I said defensively. "I slept terribly, and… Oh! I woke up around three a.m. last night. I thought I had heard a loud bang. I wasn't sure if I was dreaming, or if someone had slammed a door…"

"Or if someone had fired a gun." Reyes finished for me. "We'll be talking to the other guests, too. You're probably not the only one who heard it. Hopefully, we can find out who did this in short order. We'll need to talk to the Daltons, as well."

I dropped my head into my hand, silently chastising myself. I had been sitting there, drinking my coffee and whiling away the time until Reyes arrived, and not once had I thought to call Mama and Benny. "I'll call them right now," I said.

"I appreciate it. I'm heading to the room to cordon it off. Don't go far."

As I brought my phone to my ear and waited for Mama to answer, I said a silent prayer of thanks that Reyes trusted me. As many times as he had found me smack-dab in the middle of a murder case over the past few months, I was lucky he didn't think I was involved in any of them. Well, he had once brought me in on assault accusations, but that had quickly been cleared up. I was beginning to wonder if Nightmare had been such a deadly place before my arrival.

Mama answered groggily on the fourth ring. "Olivia?" she croaked.

"You and Benny need to get here right away," I said. "Leonard Evers was murdered in his room last night."

I had never heard Mama swear before, and it was clear my news had woken her completely. "Ten minutes." She hung up the phone without another word.

Not knowing what else to do with myself, I walked back to Leonard's room. Officer Reyes had strung yellow crime scene tape in a wide arc, blocking off the room as well as a long stretch of the walkway in front of the room. The water still flowed down over the doorstep, like a tiny waterfall.

When Reyes spied me, he walked over. "A team is on

the way to investigate. In the meantime, why don't you tell me who you think did this? After all, you've become Nightmare's amateur detective."

I waved toward the rooms nearest us. "Leonard spent two nights yelling and keeping half this place awake. I know at least one neighbor has been shouting right back at him, including a threat to call the police. But I didn't hear a peep from Leonard last night." *At least,* I added to myself, *not after his return to the motel.*

"People don't usually murder someone for talking too loudly," Reyes pointed out.

"Yeah, that's true. You might want to have a chat with Sammy Simms. He did some work in Leonard's room the other day, and later, I saw Leonard in the front office, telling Mama that Sammy had stolen some family heirlooms from him. Fancy jewelry, he said."

Reyes nodded. "I'll check to see if a police report was filed. If the victim did report the theft, then it didn't happen while I was on duty."

Reluctantly, I added, "Leonard also showed up at the Sanctuary last night." The last thing I wanted to do was drag my friends into this, but there had been so many witnesses that the police were likely to learn that tidbit, anyway. There was no point delaying the inevitable.

Reyes pursed his lips. "I don't suppose he was there just to enjoy an evening of being frightened?"

"No." I briefly explained Leonard's connection to Vivian, but I assured Reyes that he had been escorted off our property in short order. "And," I concluded, "no one at the Sanctuary was involved in his murder."

Reyes had been writing my answers in a notebook, and he stopped to gaze at me thoughtfully. "I'm quick to look there when anything strange happens in this town, but this time, you're probably right," he agreed.

As we had been talking, a few people had emerged

from their rooms, and they were now standing nearby, staring open-mouthed toward the flooded room. "What happened, Officer?" someone called to Reyes.

"We're not prepared to make a statement at this time," he answered stiffly.

That only made the onlookers more curious. When I saw two more people rushing up out of the corner of my eye, I realized it wasn't more guests but Mama and Benny. Mama had thrown on a bathrobe over her pajamas, and she was wearing flip-flops. Benny was dressed in gray sweatpants and a threadbare T-shirt.

"Sue, get the water main," Benny instructed. As Mama turned and headed toward the back of the wing, Benny looked at Reyes grimly. "What can I do to help?"

"We'll need to know everything we can about the victim, and we'll need to question everyone who was here last night in case they witnessed anything."

Benny nodded once, then glanced at me. He reached out and gave my hand a squeeze. "You found him, I suppose. How awful."

You've got that right, I thought. As Benny and Reyes continued talking, I walked a short distance away. I made it to the foot of the staircase leading to my apartment before my knees wobbled. I turned and sat down hard on the bottom step.

The shock was starting to wear off. I wrapped my arms around my knees and put my head down, hiding my face from the growing crowd in the parking lot.

Leonard had said it would be my fault if he died, and there he was, shot in his motel room.

I sat up at that thought. It wasn't my fault Leonard was dead. It was the killer's fault. But who had shot Leonard, and why? And why had the room been flooded? I thought back and realized I had heard flowing water when I had gone inside the room. The bathtub had probably been running, though what that had to do with the murder was absolutely beyond me.

It was possible Leonard had expected to be a target, and maybe he had wanted to consult with Vivian the night before to find out if there was a way to keep himself safe. I could see how someone who felt like they were in danger might turn to a psychic to discuss their future.

I would have to ask Vivian about it that night at work. In the meantime, I was more concerned with the people who were just steps away from me. Mama had rejoined Benny, who was still talking to Reyes, and she had a dazed expression on her face. I stood up slowly and made my way over to them.

"Oh, don't be ridiculous," Mama was saying to Reyes. "I've had a fair number of guests yell at me for one reason or another over the years, but I've never felt the need to kill any of them."

Reyes held up a hand. "I'm not accusing you, Mama. Goodness, do you really think I'd do that? I'm just trying to get as much detail as I can about what the victim was doing and who he was talking to leading up to his murder."

Mama's chest heaved as she took a deep breath. "Sorry, Luis. I'm just upset that someone was murdered at our motel." She glanced around at the crowd, which had grown to at least twenty people. "I don't want our guests to feel unsafe."

"We should probably let everyone know there's no water for the moment," Benny said thoughtfully, following Mama's gaze.

"You can turn it back on," said an officer who stepped up to Reyes's side. "The bathtub faucet was running full blast. All we had to do was turn off the taps."

Benny put his arm around Mama's shoulders and squeezed. "At least there's not a big leak we have to pay for," he said. It was clear he was trying to be encouraging, despite the horrible situation. He didn't quite pull it off, but Mama seemed to appreciate the effort. She tilted her head until it was resting on Benny's shoulder.

"I'll go turn the water back on," she mumbled. "You're right. We don't have to worry about fixing a pipe. But we do have to worry about replacing the carpet and furniture, and we'll probably have to replaster the walls. I'm sure the water is soaking right up into them. The neighboring rooms might need to be repaired, too, and—"

"Susie, we have insurance. It will be fine." Benny gave Mama's shoulders another squeeze.

Mama's face crumpled, and she looked like she was fighting back tears. "It's not fine. Someone was murdered here. At our motor lodge."

My heart broke for Mama. Cowboy's Corral was supposed to be a safe, welcoming place, and now, one of the guests had been shot in his room.

Benny sighed. "We have insurance," he said again. "Good thing, too. Our motel in the middle of the desert has become waterfront property."

CHAPTER SIX

I groaned loudly enough that Mama's expression immediately switched from dismayed to curious. "Olivia?" she prompted in a thick voice.

"Nothing." I shook my head hastily. "I'm just upset about all this, too."

Mama gave me a keen look that said she didn't believe one word I was saying. I knew she got strong—and usually accurate—impressions from people, and the vibe I was giving off at the moment was probably the *liar, liar, pants on fire* one.

"Can I go?" I asked Reyes.

"Yeah. We'll call you if we have follow-up questions."

I told Mama and Benny to holler if they needed anything, then got myself up my steps and into my apartment as quickly as I could. I locked the door behind me, then stood there and stared at it. I wasn't seeing the door, though. Rather, I was seeing myself at the Sanctuary, telling Damien I wanted Leonard to find a nice waterfront property and leave Nightmare forever.

A flooded motel room hadn't been the kind of waterfront property I had been picturing.

And when I had said I wished for Leonard to leave Nightmare forever, I certainly hadn't meant I wanted him to exit this world entirely.

"He said it would be my fault," I said out loud. "I conjured his murder."

A feeling of terror flooded through me. Damien had been right that I had a powerful supernatural ability, and if left unchecked, it could be dangerous. *I* could be dangerous.

I brought my hands up and rubbed my temples. "No, Liv. You're being utterly ridiculous."

I hadn't conjured a murder by magic. Someone had wanted Leonard dead, and that had absolutely nothing to do with me.

That seemed to be a much more reasonable explanation, but I still wanted to chat with Damien about the whole thing. I looked at my watch. It wasn't even ten o'clock yet. It had been the longest day ever, and yet I could still walk over to The Lusty Lunch Counter and get breakfast.

That, I realized, was a very good idea. I could head over there for a bite to eat, though I would skip breakfast and go right for my usual cheeseburger. I wasn't hungry, but I knew getting away from the motel—*the crime scene!* my brain shouted at me—would be good for me. I could get some exercise and fresh air, and I would be in a place where there hadn't been a murder.

Okay, there *had* been a murder at The Lusty, but it wasn't as fresh as this one.

I swapped my travel mug for my purse and headed out. When I got downstairs, I was relieved to see the crowd had dispersed. In fact, there was only one person still watching the police work. A man wearing a tailored black suit was standing just outside the line of yellow tape, staring intently toward the open door of Leonard's room.

Creepy.

I purposely passed close to the man. His fashion sense could give Damien a run for his money, and his short dreadlocks looked immaculate. "Good morning," I said to him.

There was no response for a beat, then the man turned and stared at me with his soft brown eyes. "It's really not," he said.

"Did you know him?" I jerked my head in the direction of Leonard's room.

"I didn't realize motel guests usually got to know each other." The man returned his gaze to the doorway. "It's still in there."

"It?"

The man's voice was just above a whisper as he answered, "The body."

Leonard had been dead for only a matter of hours, and he was already an "it." I felt kind of sorry for the guy. "Maybe you shouldn't stay here and watch if it upsets you," I suggested.

"Maybe," the man said vaguely. His attention was focused on the room again, his shoulders rigid as he watched the proceedings. With a shrug, I continued on my way.

Just stepping foot off the motel property made me feel better. I didn't feel good, but I definitely felt better.

A lot of times, I avoided High Noon Boulevard because I didn't want to wade through the hordes of tourists who were always crowding the Wild West street. Nightmare's city leaders had been smart to restore the street to what it had looked like during the copper rush in the late eighteen hundreds, even going so far as to cover the paved street in dirt so it would look period appropriate. People flocked to Nightmare to live out their own Wild West adventure.

That morning, I strolled down the covered boardwalk, still in a bit of a daze. I deftly dodged people who were stopping to take photos with two actors dressed as cowboys. They were standing near the entrance to the saloon, and tinny piano music wafted from beyond the short swinging doors. One of the cowboys winked at me as I walked past. "Mornin', ma'am. You be careful. There's a criminal in town."

I stopped short. "You already heard?" I asked, surprised.

The man's friendly smile faltered slightly, but then he said, "Sure have. The whole town is buzzing with the news that Butch Tanner has come back to Nightmare."

Oh. Of course. This guy, I reminded myself, was an actor pretending to be someone from more than a century before. Even if he had heard about the murder at the motel, he wasn't going to chat about it casually while he was in character. Instead, he was hyping up the upcoming reenactment that would happen between the actors playing Butch Tanner and Connor McCrory. The outlaw and the sheriff had famously killed each other in a shootout in the middle of High Noon Boulevard, back in the late eighteen hundreds.

I leaned conspiratorially toward the cowboy. "When I see McCrory, I'll let him know he needs to be on high alert." I chuckled at my own inside joke as I walked away, since chances were good I would see McCrory at work that night. He and Tanner haunted the Sanctuary.

The short interchange did me even more good than the walk and the fresh air. By the time I walked into The Lusty Lunch Counter, I was prepared for the barrage of questions I would get. Because, in a town as small as Nightmare, I knew the news of the murder had already reached the diner. It was the hub of town gossip.

I hopped onto a stool at the stainless steel counter, and less than a minute later, my usual server, Ella, was sliding a diet soda toward me. She leaned over the counter, her big hoop earrings swinging with the movement. When she just stared at me, I finally said, "What?" I self-consciously reached a hand up to pat my hair, ensuring it wasn't sticking out in crazy directions.

"What do you mean, what?" Ella countered. "You live at Cowboy's Corral. You must have seen something."

"I had a front-row seat." I took a long sip of my soda while Ella continued to eyeball me expectantly. "I found him."

Ella's expression turned to one of concern, and she reached out to put a hand over mine. "Olivia, I'm so sorry. I didn't know. Are you okay?"

I started to nod but stopped myself. There was no point lying about it. "No, I'm not okay. Leonard was a difficult guest, but I can't imagine who would have wanted him dead. And you know what? I'm tired of finding dead bodies around this town."

Ella looked thoughtful for a moment. "Yeah, me, too. I've only found one, and that was more than enough. You've found…two now, right?"

"Three, if you count Kelly Lowry. But no one found her, exactly. She was just onstage for all of us in the audience to see." Ella still had her hand over mine, and I turned my wrist so I could grasp her fingers. "I've been wondering: were there this many murders before I came to Nightmare?"

"No. Nightmare wasn't always like this."

Maybe it's me, then. Am I conjuring murders in my new town?

"It's not you," Ella said, seeming to read my mind.

I grimaced. "Thanks. I actually needed to hear that."

Ella gave me a wink. "A cheeseburger will cheer you up. I'll go put in your order."

As I waited for my food, I spun slowly around on my stool to look at the diners packed into the booths. The place looked so fun and retro, with red upholstery and a black-and-white tile floor, but I wondered how many of the conversations happening around the diner were about the murder. The two men sitting on one side of me seemed to be discussing an upcoming trip, and the booth directly across from me included two children.

Maybe I would have a peaceful lunch, after all.

Ella slid a plate with a cheeseburger and a mountain of fries on it in front of me just a few minutes later. I had just taken my first bite when I felt a light brush against my arm. I glanced over to see Emmett Kline climbing ungracefully onto the empty stool next to me. "Sorry, Olivia. Hope I didn't bump you too hard."

I swallowed quickly and said, "No, I barely felt it. You doing all right, Emmett?" He looked harried, and I noticed his tie was slightly askew. Emmett always looked well put together, so his appearance was clearly a sign something was going on.

"I just lost a client," Emmett said ruefully. He waved at Ella, and when she saw him, he made a motion with his hand like he was drinking a cup of coffee. Ella gave him a thumbs-up, and as she bustled over with a white mug and a pot of coffee, he continued, "It was looking like he might make me a lot of money. Such a disappointment."

I looked at Emmett sympathetically, even though I wanted to laugh. Emmett was known for being a bit of a ruthless real estate agent. He was all about the money and what he could get out of a deal. Despite that, I kind of liked the guy. "Sorry to hear it. What happened?"

"That murder, of course," Emmett said, as if it were obvious. "Leonard Evers had a lot of money, if his taste in real estate was any indication."

This time, I did laugh, but it was an outburst of disbelief, not humor. "So he really was looking for a place to live in Nightmare?"

"Yeah. He wanted to settle down out West. Such a

shame. That commission check would have been real nice." Emmett shook his head.

Leave it to Emmett to be more concerned about his bank account than a murder victim. I picked up a french fry and waved it toward Emmett. "A new client will come along soon enough. You'll be fine."

"You're right. In fact, I got a new client just yesterday. I try not to judge a person by their wardrobe, but his suit was nicer than anything in my closet, and that's saying a lot. He might just be more lucrative for me than Leonard. Maybe you've met him? He says he checked into Cowboy's Corral yesterday. Hopefully, his taste in real estate is as expensive as his taste in clothes!"

CHAPTER SEVEN

Emmett looked at me with a self-satisfied expression, and I knew he was seeing not me but dollar signs.

I raised an eyebrow, my fry forgotten for the moment. "Your new client is a snappy dresser, huh? I haven't met him yet, but I think I saw him—" I stopped before I could add, "at the crime scene."

"I have high hopes for Brian." Emmett actually brought the tips of his fingers together, and all he needed was a black pencil mustache to look like the perfect villain.

No wonder I once thought he was a murderer.

"Brian, huh?" I tried to sound casual. "He's looking for a new home in Nightmare, just like Leonard was?"

"He says he's shopping around for investment properties. I told him about the luxury cabins I'm planning to build at Barker Ranch, and he's interested in supporting the project."

"Hmm," was all I answered. It seemed odd that two men showed up at Cowboy's Corral, both looking for local real estate, at about the same time. Was there a connection between Leonard and Brian, or was it just a coincidence? The way Brian had been staring into Leonard's room had been unsettling, and I wondered if the killer had returned to the scene of the crime to enjoy his handiwork.

Emmett wagged a finger at me. "You can be as judgmental as you like, but those cabins are going to be incredibly popular with tourists looking for a nice mountain getaway!"

"I'm not judging your ambitions, Emmett. Barker Ranch has spectacular views, and I agree, the cabins will probably be booked solid once they're built."

"If you're not judging me like everyone else in this town does, then why do you have that look on your face?"

I shrugged. "Leonard's room is below mine, and somebody went in there last night and killed him. And you wonder why I might have a strange expression?"

Emmett patted my arm. "I hadn't stopped to consider how close you were to the crime. I'm glad you're okay."

"Me, too," I said, right before I picked up my cheeseburger and took a giant bite. I figured it was the most polite way of telling Emmett I was ready to stop talking about the murder. He took the hint, and while I ate, he sipped his coffee and told me about some land by the interstate that he wanted to buy. I nodded affably and made the appropriate "mm-hmm" noises, even though I was only half listening. Instead, I was thinking about Brian, the well-dressed man who might be involved in a murder.

As I walked back to my apartment after lunch, I was still mulling over the idea that Brian might have killed Leonard. I mentally checked off the evidence against him. One, he and Leonard had both come to Nightmare in search of real estate. Two, he had arrived at the motel just the day before, according to Emmett. Could Leonard's talk of death at the Sanctuary have been prompted by Brian's arrival? And, for my third piece of evidence, Brian had been staring awfully intently at the crime scene.

When I listed it out like that, I realized how vague that "evidence" really was. I had seen enough crime scenes in the past two months that I was probably getting somewhat used to seeing them, so I didn't feel the need to stand and stare at the spectacle. Brian, on the other hand, probably had fewer dead bodies popping up in his life. I couldn't blame him for being curious about a murder in the very place he was staying.

I still thought Leonard's dire warning about his death might be tied to Brian's arrival, though. I would have to talk to Vivian some more. Maybe, now that Leonard was dead, she wouldn't mind sharing what they had discussed when he had visited her on Saturday morning. And even if she didn't want to discuss it with me, she might have to divulge details to the police.

A feeling of dread washed over me as I reached the motel and saw the police tape was still in place. A police van was parked just outside Leonard's room. I guess some part of me had hoped the whole thing would be wrapped up by the time I got back from lunch. I didn't want to spend my afternoon sitting in my apartment, right above an active crime scene, but I also knew taking my laptop up to the front office wasn't a good idea. Mama and Benny would have their hands full, and my presence would only be a distraction.

So, instead, I packed up my laptop and the charging cable, then walked back over to High Noon Boulevard. I headed straight for The Caffeinated Cadaver, a coffee shop in what used to be Nightmare's mortuary. I hunted around the room until I found an empty wingback chair that was near a power outlet. The hulking, ancient laptop Mama had loaned me when I started working for the motel wouldn't hold a charge, so it had to be plugged in.

I was halfway through both a latte and an updated write-up about the motel for Nightmare's tourism website when a shadow fell over me. I looked up to see a man with unkempt sandy hair and gray eyes in a deeply tanned face. He was smiling down at me. "What a wild day, am I right?" he boomed happily.

I had no idea who this guy was, but he was talking to me like we knew each other. Figuring I could use the "I'm new here and can't keep up with all the people I've met" excuse, I cleared my throat and said politely, "I'm so sorry, but please remind me of your name."

The man laughed, the corners of his eyes crinkling. "We've never met!"

"Gabe, are you harassing strangers again?" called a voice from somewhere behind the man who, I assumed, was Gabe. A woman appeared at his side. She had squeezed herself into a midnight-blue corset that looked about two sizes too small, and below that, I spied plenty of bare leg between the hemline of her short black skirt and her black cowboy boots.

The woman flipped her long brown hair over her shoulder. "Sorry," she said with a grin. "Normally I keep him on his leash!"

"No problem," I mumbled. Eyeing her ensemble, I asked, "Do you work at the saloon?"

"Oh, you like my outfit?" The woman twirled around. Once she was facing me again, she said, "We're just visiting Nightmare, and I wanted to dress the part. Ooh, I've been dying to ask a local about an urban legend here. Is it true that—"

"June, don't you recognize her?" Gabe interrupted. "She's not a local. She's staying at the same motel as us."

Ah-ha! So that's why he seems to know me. "But we've never met, as you mentioned," I said to Gabe.

"I saw you talking to the police this morning." Gabe leaned toward me and brought one hand to the side of his mouth. In a loud whisper, he said, "I also saw you in the parking lot around one in the morning, the night before our dear neighbor was killed. You weren't stalking him, I hope."

I couldn't manage even a hint of a smile as Gabe

laughed at his own joke. "I was just getting home from work," I explained. Something clicked in my head, and I said, "You're the one who was shouting at Leonard to quiet down, weren't you?"

Gabe spread his hands wide and bowed. "I am. And how fortunate that he's been quieted. I expect we'll all sleep better tonight!"

He wasn't wrong that everyone at Cowboy's Corral could expect a peaceful night, but it was still an awful thing to say. I decided right then and there that I did not care for Gabe one bit. I glanced at June again. The jury was still out on her.

"Come on, Gabe, I need coffee before we go watch the shootout! Get out some of that cash you just made and buy me a mint mocha iced coffee!" June tugged on Gabe's hand.

"See ya, neighbor!" Gabe said. "Don't come after me tonight. I promise we'll be quiet!" With a grin that looked both silly and sinister, Gabe turned and let June lead him to the counter.

I stared at my laptop screen after that, watching the two of them in my peripheral vision. I really wanted to know what June had meant about Gabe having just made some cash. I couldn't help but think back to Leonard saying his valuables had been stolen. Maybe Sammy the plumber hadn't taken them, but Gabe.

Or, maybe, I was just looking for connections where there were none. I reminded myself that Gabe's lack of empathy about Leonard's murder shouldn't be suspicious. He hadn't known the guy beyond shouting at him.

I'd been around enough murders lately that my brain was in overdrive trying to figure out who had a motive and who didn't. "Silly," I told myself as I watched June swagger out the door, Gabe trailing behind her and laughing at something.

But, no matter how silly I felt, I still added Gabe to my list of suspects. Could someone be so annoyed by a loud neighbor that they would kill over it? I supposed it was possible, but I also figured it was unlikely. It was June's mention of Gabe's influx of cash that had landed him a spot on my list.

As the afternoon wore on, I realized I was reluctant to go home. Being away from the motel felt more comfortable than being in my own apartment. After my latte, I made it through a cappuccino, an iced coffee, and even a blueberry scone. I was buzzing from both caffeine and sugar, but I still didn't want to leave.

My watch, however, told me I had to go home to get ready for work that night at the Sanctuary.

At least going home that time around was better, since there was no sign of emergency vehicles in the motel's parking lot. The yellow crime scene tape still stood sentinel around Leonard's room, though.

After I changed into jeans and a Nightmare Sanctuary Haunted House T-shirt, I stopped by the front office before walking to work. Only Benny was there, and when he stood up to greet me, I could see the weariness on his face. I realized that, at some point during the day, he had changed out of his pajamas, at least.

"I sent Sue home to get some rest," he said in greeting. "You look like you could use some yourself."

"I'm beat, but I have work tonight." I leaned on the countertop and peered at Benny's face. "Is there someone else who can come and cover for you? You should be at home with Mama."

"I'm better off keeping an eye on this place," Benny countered. "And maybe you're better off at Nightmare Sanctuary than at home, too. It's been a long afternoon for those folks, as I understand."

CHAPTER EIGHT

I folded my arms on the countertop and rested my head on them. My voice sounded muffled as I addressed the Formica. "The police," I said.

"I hear they've been over there at the Sanctuary, grilling folks about Mr. Evers," Benny said. "Did you see him there at the haunted house last night?"

I raised my head, propping my chin on my arms. "Yeah. I'm the one who told the police he had been there." I felt like someone had hollowed out my chest. "Benny, did I make a mistake? Was I wrong to tell the police that Leonard went there?"

Benny bent at the waist slightly, until his eyes were level with mine. "You did the right thing. You told the police the truth."

"Maybe I should have left out that part of the truth."

"This town isn't always fair to the folks out at the haunted house." Benny didn't need to tell me that. It was something I had learned on my first full day in Nightmare. "But we have to trust that the police are looking for justice, not a scapegoat."

"You're right. It didn't work when Luke Dawes tried to frame someone at the Sanctuary for Jared Barker's murder."

"Exactly. You have nothing to fear. In fact, imagine if

you hadn't told the police that detail. They would have heard about Mr. Evers going there from someone else, and that would have made your omission seem awfully suspicious. The police might have thought you were covering for yourself or one of your co-workers. Getting it all out in the open was the best, safest thing for you to do."

Benny was making perfect sense, but I still had that hollow feeling, and I was surprised to feel tears forming in my eyes. "But what if they're mad at me for telling?" I whispered.

"Then they're not your friends," Benny said firmly.

I bit my lip. Usually, I looked forward to going to work. And, after the events at the motel, work would be a welcome distraction. Or it should have been. Instead, though, I was suddenly filled with dread.

Benny put a hand on my head, like a father comforting a child. "They'll understand, Olivia. And if they don't, you have my permission to give them what for!"

That elicited a smile from me, and I stood up straight. "Thanks, Benny. I hope tomorrow is better than today."

"It will be. You have fun at work."

I drove to work instead of walking. One moment, I would stomp on the gas pedal, anxious to get there and see if my friends were mad at me for sending the police in their direction. The next, I would slow to a crawl, trying to avoid the encounter.

After I parked, I walked in much the same way as I approached the double front doors under the portico. The moon had wrapped up its three days at full, which meant Zach was back in his human form. He already had the ticket window open, and I could see him there on my right, just inside the window, but I purposely fixed my eyes on the doors. Zach was notorious for being grumpy, and he was always in an especially bad mood when he had to return to what he thought of as his boring life as a human.

I grabbed a door handle just as Zach called my name. Reluctantly, I turned. "Yeah?" I asked timidly.

"Come here," Zach said impatiently.

The short distance between the doors and the ticket window felt like a mile as I approached. Zach leaned forward over the little countertop fitted onto the bottom of the window. "I'm really sorry," he said.

I blinked at him. "No, I'm sorry."

"For what?"

"For bringing the police down on this place. I told them Leonard had been here last night, asking for Vivian. I'm so sorry. I know no one likes it when the Sanctuary is under a microscope, and—"

"Olivia, are you apologizing for telling the police the truth?" Zach was smiling at me lopsidedly.

"Um… Yes?"

Zach gazed toward the ceiling and shook his head, his long rust-red hair falling over his shoulders. "You are so silly sometimes." He dropped his gaze to me, his expression serious. "You did the right thing. We were all able to provide alibis for the time of the murder, and Malcolm and Clara backed up what you said about Leonard shouting at you. Yeah, we were under a microscope, but it was over within a few hours."

I felt my shoulders relax. "Oh, thank goodness," I said. I could feel the dread dissipating.

"But back to what I said before. I'm sorry."

"For what?"

"You found another dead body today. Where you live, no less." Zach shrugged. "I'm sorry you had to go through that again."

"Thanks. I'm hanging in there." I hesitated for a moment, then said, "So no one here is mad at me?"

"Not that I know of. Damien will probably say some-thing mean, but that's every day." Zach grinned.

"I'd better go get it over with, then." I went inside feeling a lot less trepidation. I turned right as soon as I walked through the front entrance and headed down the hallway toward Damien's office.

The door to the office was open, so I knocked on the frame as I walked in. I had thought the dread was gone, but as soon as I saw Damien, I blurted, "Please don't yell at me."

Damien had been focused on the laptop on his desk, and he looked up at me with drawn eyebrows. His voice was quiet as he said, "Is that really what you think of me? That I would start yelling because our visitor last night turned up dead?"

I averted my eyes, focusing instead on a built-in bookcase to my left. "No. Because I told the police he turned up here before he turned up dead."

"Olivia…"

"I'm being silly, I know." I was still standing in the doorway, and I forced myself to walk forward. "Zach said the same thing. I just worried you'd be mad that the police came out here because of me."

"The only secret you have to keep is that we harbor supernatural creatures here. I would never ask you to lie to the police. You can't tell them everything if it would give us away, but lie? Never. You did the right thing."

Benny had said the same thing. So had Zach. And yet, it wasn't until I heard it the third time that it finally, truly sank in. I collapsed into one of the chairs, buried my face in my hands, and started to cry. I mentally kicked myself for crying in front of Damien, but I couldn't help it. All the shock, stress, and fear of the day had piled up, and the proverbial dam had finally broken.

I felt Damien perch on the armrest of my chair, and his arm slid around my shoulders. When he spoke, I could tell he was leaning down, his head close to mine. His voice was gentle. "You don't have to work tonight. You can go home and get some rest."

I sniffed loudly and sat up. "No. I don't want to go home. I'd rather be here." I wiped at my eyes with both hands. "I think I'll be better now that I've gotten that out of my system."

Damien's arm slid away from me as he stood and returned to his desk chair. "Do you…want to stay here for a while?" I could hear the awkwardness, and I realized Damien probably wasn't used to being a shoulder to cry on.

"No, but…" I steeled myself and looked into Damien's eyes. "I think it might be my fault Leonard is dead." I laid out my wish about him finding waterfront property, and Benny's comment that Leonard's room had become exactly that.

When I was done, Damien shook his head. "You wished for him to find waterfront property, not for him to die. That comment you overheard is just a coincidence."

I laughed sardonically. "Let's hope so."

"By the way," Damien began, "I found something at the mine today. There was a fresh-cut rose lying on the ground at the front door. I have no idea who would have left it there, or why."

"Maybe someone accidentally dropped it there, or"—I searched for some other suggestion—"it blew out of the back of a truck?"

"I find both of those options unlikely."

"Just another mystery about your dad's mine," I said.

Before Damien could respond, I heard a voice behind me say, "What about the mine?" I knew it was Vivian.

"Someone left a rose at the front door," Damien said.

"Interesting." Vivian sat down in the chair next to mine. "I was hoping to find you here, Olivia. I kept the details of Leonard's reading vague when I talked to the police, but I want to give you all the details."

I tilted my head quizzically. "Why didn't you want to tell the police everything?"

Vivian waved a hand. "The full story delves into supernatural stuff. The police probably wouldn't have believed me, so it seemed pointless to tell them."

"Are they details that might help us find Leonard's killer?" I asked.

"Probably not." Vivian's expression turned sad. "Actually, I'm worried his death is partly my fault. I had told him he was safe."

"Safe from what?"

Vivian gripped the arms of her chair. "Leonard came to me because he'd had a vision of his death. I told him there was no way he could experience what he had seen as long as he was in Nightmare. He had seen himself dying on the waterfront."

CHAPTER NINE

Vivian laughed wryly. "What a huge mistake I've made! I told Leonard he would be perfectly safe in Nightmare, as long as he stayed away from the only waterfront around here, which is Copper Creek. When the police told me about the flooding in his motel room, I knew his vision had actually come to pass."

"You can't blame yourself, Vivian," I said.

"I didn't even bother to consult the spirits or tune into my sixth sense. I just reassured him because it was logical. You can't die on the waterfront if there's no waterfront! If I had only made an effort to see his fate, maybe Leonard would still be alive."

I reached over and put a hand on Vivian's arm. "You can't blame yourself," I repeated, "because it's my fault he's dead."

"No, it isn't," Damien said tersely.

"I wished for him to find waterfront property, and there was a flood in his room! I conjured the setting Leonard saw in his vision. If I hadn't created the waterfront, then he wouldn't have died." I stood abruptly, too agitated to remain seated. "And don't tell me again that it was just a coincidence! What are the chances my wish would just so happen to match Leonard's vision?"

Damien turned from me to Vivian. Quietly, he told her, "Go get the witches."

I sat down again, fighting the urge to cry for the second time that night. Damien didn't say a word. He probably realized arguing with me would be pointless. Part of me wanted to yell at him for making me believe I might actually be a conjuror. If he hadn't been telling me over and over that I had that ability, then I wouldn't be blaming myself for a murder.

A few minutes later, Vivian returned. I turned and saw Maida, Madge, and Morgan gliding into Damien's office behind her. Maida, the witch who looked like she was only a child, bounded over to me and took my hand. "Miss Olivia is upset," she announced in her high voice.

"She's had a shock," Morgan agreed. Her wispy white hair floated around her face, and her wrinkles stood out sharply in the light of the office.

"She's had a revelation," Madge corrected. "How can we help?"

"I want to know if you can determine how powerful Olivia is," Damien said. "Is there a spell you can do that will uncover how strong her conjuring skills are?"

"If only it were that easy, my boy," Morgan said. "If such a spell existed, we would have cast it on you years ago."

"To find out how powerful *you* really are," Maida agreed.

"But such a spell doesn't exist," Madge finished. "All we can say is that Olivia radiates an enormous energy. She has passion and tenacity."

"But is it power? Is she a conjuror?" Morgan shook her head. "There is no way to know for certain until she exhibits those skills beyond a doubt."

"That's the problem," I mumbled. "It's possible I

already did exhibit them, and someone is dead because of it."

Maida squeezed my hand. "Sorry we can't help, Miss Olivia."

"Thank you, ladies," Damien said. "You can go. All of you. The meeting has probably already started."

The witches all looked at me sympathetically before leaving, and Vivian followed after them once she told me confidently, "We'll figure it all out."

Once it was just Damien and me, I smiled sadly at him. "Did you think that was going to make me feel better?"

"I thought they might be able to tell you whether you were even capable of conjuring a murder. And, honestly, I thought they would say your skills are still in their infancy." Damien sighed and flopped back into his chair, his head tilted upward so he could stare at the ceiling. "My plan to reassure you has backfired spectacularly."

"At least they called me tenacious instead of stubborn." I laughed weakly.

Damien tilted his head down and leaned forward, resting his elbows on the desk as he looked at me earnestly. "Find the killer," he said firmly. "Solve this murder. Not for Mama. Not for the dead guy. For yourself. Prove that someone else is to blame for this, and that your skills had nothing to do with it."

"Maybe I wished so hard to get Leonard out of Cowboy's Corral that I magically made someone murder him. Even if I do find the killer, I could still be responsible for Leonard's death."

"I think what you'll find is that a lot of things were already in motion long before you even knew who Leonard was. His murder was just the latest in a chain of events that you had nothing to do with."

I swallowed hard. "If that's the truth, then it would make me feel better."

Damien stood and came around the desk, so he was standing right in front of me. He reached out a hand, and when I took it, he pulled me into a standing position. "I know how scary it is to have a power you don't understand," he said softly. "It's why I've been trying to help you learn to control it. But right now, finding the killer and knowing the truth are the only things I want your mind focused on. Okay?"

"Okay." I straightened my shoulders. "And you're right. I have been focused on not letting my emotions get too high lately. I've been better at controlling them, so if I am a conjuror, I'm less likely to accidentally manifest something. Yes, I was wishing for Leonard to find property and leave the motel, but not with the same passion and dedication you say it takes to truly conjure something. When I found the job listing for the Sanctuary, I was feeling desperate and afraid. Those emotions were far stronger than my annoyance at a loud neighbor."

"Remember that." Damien nudged me in the direction of the door. "You can catch the tail end of the staff meeting if you go now."

"Family meeting," I corrected as I headed for the door. Before I left, I turned to Damien. "Thank you."

By the time I slunk into the dining room, the family meeting was over. Mori rushed up to me. "I was worried when you didn't show up. We have thirty minutes before we open for the night. Tell me everything."

Mori just hugged me tightly after I filled her in, and she agreed with Damien that solving Leonard's murder would make me feel better. Just as Mori finished talking, I felt two arms encircle me from behind, and a voice spoke in my ear. "We're here for you, Olivia."

I reached up and squeezed Theo's forearms. His vampiric nature allowed him to sneak up on me all the time, but I wasn't going to complain about a surprise hug.

I had hoped work would be good for me, and I had been right. The support from my friends and the distraction of scaring guests alongside Theo in the lagoon vignette, where I was stationed for the night, helped me realize there was more to my life than yet another murder.

When I woke up on Monday, Damien's advice to me was the first thing I thought of. He was right; I needed to find Leonard's killer for my own sake. One of the things I really wanted to know was how Leonard's room had turned into "waterfront property" in the first place. In other words, why had his bathtub faucet been running? I supposed Leonard could have been drawing a bath for himself when his killer ambushed him, but I figured there might be more to the story.

And where best to start finding out about a water issue than with the very plumber who had just been in Leonard's room? Between the water at the crime scene, Leonard's accusations that Sammy Simms had stolen valuable jewelry from him, and Sammy's appearance in my own room, I knew he was the first person I wanted to talk to.

I looked up the address for Sammy Simms Plumbing, and before long, I was standing in front of a sagging clapboard building in a rundown area on the southeast side of Nightmare. Judging by the signs on the buildings around me, I was in an industrial area. If I needed building supplies or construction equipment, this was the neighborhood for it.

What I really needed, though, was a chat with Sammy, and it was just what I couldn't get. The grimy glass door of his office was locked up tight. I put my face close to the glass and shaded my eyes with my hands, trying to get a look inside. The lights were off, but I could make out a metal desk piled with papers. Stacks of boxes towered around it.

Sammy was probably out on a call, and I didn't want to stand there and wait all day. I considered calling him myself, but I didn't think he'd rush over to his office if I said, "I'm trying to find out if you're a murderer, so I'd like to ask you a few questions."

Besides, I realized, maybe Sammy not being in was the best possible scenario. I couldn't get into his office, but I knew who could.

In a flash, I was back in my car and on my way to the Sanctuary. When I pulled up, I was glad to see a delivery truck parked out front and Justine standing at the door, signing for a package. That meant I could get into the building without having to knock, which risked waking someone up. I wished Justine a good morning as I breezed past and made a beeline for Damien's office.

Except the door was locked. My second locked office of the day, and it wasn't even noon yet.

"You need something from in there?" Justine called down the hallway. She was standing in the entryway with a cardboard box balanced on one hip.

"I need Tanner and McCrory!"

Justine grinned, put down the box, and headed toward me. As she pulled out her keys, she said, "I don't know what you're up to, but I'll help however I can."

"I'm going to ask them to investigate a suspect in Leonard's death," I answered.

Justine unlocked the office door and opened it wide. "Look in the middle drawer of Damien's desk."

I did as Justine instructed. Inside the drawer was the small, worn wooden box that held Butch Tanner and Connor McCrory's six-shooters, the very guns they had used to kill each other in their shootout on High Noon Boulevard. The ghosts of the outlaw and the sheriff were tethered to the guns, so wherever the ghosts wanted to go, the guns had to go, too. "Tanner! McCrory!" I called. "Hey, boys!"

Justine pointed over my shoulder. "Try the call button."

Oh, right. I had seen Damien use one of the old brass buttons on the wall, which I figured was a call system that had been installed back when the building had still been Nightmare Sanctuary Hospital and Asylum. There were yellowed handwritten labels next to each button. One of the labels had the names of the ghosts, so I pressed the corresponding button. Less than ten seconds later, Tanner and McCrory sailed through a bookcase and into the room.

"Miss Olivia, Miss Justine. Good to see you both," Tanner said. His mouth and nose were hidden behind his red bandanna, but his eyes were sparkling.

McCrory's bushy black mustache twitched as he raised his black cowboy hat. "Mornin', ladies."

"Gentlemen, there's been another murder," I said. "Would you care to help me investigate a suspect?"

Tanner let out a whoop of excitement. McCrory stood up a little straighter and said, "Of course. We'll see that justice is done."

I explained everything on the drive back to Sammy's office. The six-shooter box sat on the passenger seat next to me, and the ghosts were in the back seat. I felt like some kind of chauffeur for spirits. As soon as I pulled up in front of Sammy's office, Tanner and McCrory disappeared, and I knew they were already going inside to take a look around.

I got out of my car and walked up to the front door right as McCrory came out through it, his form barely visible in the daylight. "You were right to look into this guy," he said. "There's an open box under his desk, and there's a pile of old jewelry inside it. It looks real expensive."

CHAPTER TEN

I gasped and pressed my face against the glass door again, trying to see inside. My head passed through McCrory's shoulder, sending a wave of cold through my skull. I jerked backward and sputtered, feeling like I had just dunked my head under ice-cold water.

In fact, it reminded me an awful lot of trying to rinse out my hair conditioner with the pitcher of water from my fridge.

"Can you describe the jewelry?" I asked excitedly.

"Tanner's got a good head for details of stolen goods," McCrory said with a judgmental harrumph. "He's taking an inventory, though of course, he can only catalog the things lying right there on top of the pile. Sure would be nice if we could handle evidence." To drive home his point, McCrory reached forward, his fingers disappearing into the side of my purse.

"Still, this is extremely useful information," I said, hitching my purse a little higher on my shoulder and out of McCrory's reach. It was an expensive designer bag, the last luxury item I still owned. I didn't think ghosts left ectoplasm behind—I hadn't seen any yet from my ghostly friends—but I didn't want to take my chances. "This might be proof that Sammy really did steal from Leonard, and if Sammy is a thief, then it's possible he's a killer, too."

McCrory smiled. "Maybe I'll get credit with helping bring him down. It will be the first time I've been involved in an official murder investigation in more than a hundred years."

My excitement deflated instantly. What was I supposed to do, call the police and tell them a couple of ghosts had been snooping around in Sammy's office? I certainly couldn't claim I had gone inside and found the jewelry, because that would get me arrested for trespassing or, worse, breaking and entering.

Maybe I can call in an anonymous tip.

A white pickup truck with the Sammy Simms Plumbing logo on the door pulled up as I was pondering what to do. McCrory hastily slid through the door and into the office so he wouldn't be spotted.

Sammy climbed out of the truck and walked toward me, his eyes roving back and forth. "Is there someone here with you?" he asked.

"Nope. It's just me."

Sammy tilted his head. "You're the woman whose apartment I accidentally went into over at Cowboy's Corral. What brings you out here?" I could hear the suspicion in his voice, and I couldn't blame him.

"Well…" I began, searching around for something other than the truth. I had never been good at flat-out lying, though. "I had a little run-in with Leonard—the victim—the night before he died. He was acting really odd, and I was just wondering if anyone else noticed his behavior. I know you did some plumbing work for him."

Sammy's eyes narrowed. He clearly didn't trust me, but after a moment, he said, "He was a real piece of work."

"How so?" I asked.

"He came back to his room as I was finishing up my work there, and he started shouting at me to get out. I told him I needed to finish tightening up some washers so he wouldn't have any leaks, but he wouldn't stop badgering me. He said some strange things."

"Did he seem afraid?"

"Yeah." Sammy nodded his head slowly. "He seemed nervous, and he kept going on and on about how the psychic was a fraud."

"A fraud? But he seemed to believe in Vivian's abilities."

"Who's Vivian?" Sammy asked, looking confused.

"The psychic. She works at Nightmare Sanctuary."

Sammy chuckled. "The haunted house? No, he was talking about Alana, our town psychic. Haven't you seen her place out on Route 23? It's the adobe building with the neon palm-reading sign out front."

It was my turn to laugh as I said, "I had no idea there was a town psychic! I'm fairly new here, and even though Nightmare is small, I haven't explored all of it yet."

"The guy kept saying she was a fraud, and that there was no way what she said could have been true. He seemed a bit obsessed with whatever woo-woo stuff she did to him."

"It sounds like he had a psychic fixation," I said, more to myself than to Sammy.

"The dude definitely had some issues. I have to get going to my next appointment. You, uh... You done here?"

Sammy was obviously not going to open up his office, and I wondered if it was because I was there, or if he really did have to get to his next customer. If that were the case, then why had he driven to his office in the first place? I expected he was leaving because he didn't want to risk me following him inside the office, where I might catch sight of the jewelry.

Too bad. I could have called the police and claimed to

have spotted the stolen goods while I was inside with Sammy.

Since it was clear I wasn't going to get that shot, there didn't seem to be any reason to prolong our conversation. "Thanks for talking to me," I said. "It helps."

"Helps what?"

I waved a hand in the air and tried to keep my tone casual. "It helps to know Leonard wasn't making a good impression with anyone."

Sammy had relaxed a bit as we chatted, but he stiffened again. "Why? Are you trying to figure out who killed him, or something?"

I didn't answer, but my lopsided grimace must have made it clear because Sammy began to back away from me. "Leave the police to their work," he said. "You don't want to wind up in trouble like he did." With that, Sammy hopped back into his truck and drove away, leaving me to stare after him with my mouth wide open. I wasn't sure if he was trying to help me or threaten me.

"You catchin' flies?" Tanner drawled.

I turned to see that he and McCrory had joined me. "Hopefully, I'm catching a thief and a killer," I quipped. "Let's go."

It was only after we were back in my car and on the road that I realized how stupid it had been for me to go to Sammy's office by myself. Of course, I wasn't exactly alone, but if there had been any trouble, Tanner and McCrory couldn't have done anything other than give Sammy the chills.

"Miss Olivia, are you listening?" Tanner asked.

I snapped back to the present moment and glanced in my rearview mirror. "Sorry, Tanner. Were you saying something?"

Tanner sighed dramatically. "This is why women can't be lawmen," he grumbled. "Too flighty."

"Excuse me?" I said. I tried to twist around in my seat so I could glare at Tanner, but I veered violently toward the center lines. I had to keep my eyes on the road as I lectured, "I'll have you know that there are many women in law enforcement, and they are excellent at their jobs!"

McCrory laughed loudly. "Tanner, don't you remember those Arizona Rangers who came out to the Sanctuary a few years ago? They were tracking someone who was trying to escape justice. They had a lady, and she looked right nice in her uniform. In fact, her hat looked a lot like mine."

I shook my head disapprovingly. "Tanner, why don't you get back to what you were telling me?"

"I was saying that the jewelry looked nice. There were two ruby necklaces, one emerald bracelet, and earrings made from diamonds and pearls. Real nice stuff." I could hear the desire in Tanner's voice. That would have been a good haul for him back in his outlaw days.

"That is some nice jewelry. If it really is Leonard's, then no wonder he was so upset when it went missing," I said.

When we got back to the Sanctuary, Zach was just coming around the corner of the building as I walked up to the front entrance. He was making a lap of the grounds as part of his work as the Sanctuary's security guard, and while he seemed surprised to see me, he seemed even more surprised that Tanner and McCrory were with me.

"What have you been up to?" Zach asked me, eyeing the ghosts.

"Do you really want to know?"

Zach shook his head. "No. I'm sure you're getting yourself into some kind of trouble, and it has something to do with that dead man."

"You're very perceptive. Are you sure you're not a

psychic?" I held out the six-shooter box. "Can you please give this to Damien?"

Zach took the box, and I thanked Tanner and McCrory before heading out. Joking with Zach about being psychic had reminded me about Alana, the woman Sammy had referred to as the town psychic. I also recalled that Justine had mentioned Vivian didn't advertise her services because she didn't want to step on the toes of Nightmare's resident psychic. At some point, I knew, I should talk to Alana to find out anything I could about her encounter with Leonard.

First, though, I wanted to talk to Vivian so I could know as much about Alana as possible. Since Vivian was probably asleep like so many of the other Sanctuary residents, I would have to wait. In the meantime, I wasn't sure what to do with myself. I didn't want to be confined to my apartment, and I also didn't want to sit in the front office of the motel. I needed to check on Mama and Benny, though I figured I would do that later. At the moment, they were probably busy sorting out the water damage to Leonard's room.

It was lunchtime, but I didn't feel all that hungry yet. Besides, even though I wasn't broke like I had been when I had first arrived in Nightmare, I was still on a budget. I had just eaten at The Lusty Lunch Counter the day before, so I needed to fix myself something at home. Which was where I didn't want to go.

I sighed and started to drive, still not sure where I was going. When I reached the main road that ran through Nightmare, I turned left, away from the motel and High Noon Boulevard. As I wound my way north, I realized I was heading in the direction of Done Right Auto Repair.

I pulled up in front of the whitewashed building to see that the doors of both service bays were wide open. Nick was working on a pickup truck in one of the bays, his white overalls streaked with oil and grease. "Hey, Nick!" I called as I climbed out of my car.

Nick straightened up and waved a wrench in greeting. "What's wrong with your car?"

"Nothing. I just came out here——"

I was saved by having to come up with a valid excuse for my visit by Nick's daughter, Lucy. "Miss Olivia is here!" she yelled as she ran toward me, her mass of dark curls bouncing. "Are you going to take me to the haunted house again? It's October now, and I'm going to have the coolest Halloween costume ever. My grandma is making it for me." Lucy wrapped her arms around my waist.

I always admired Lucy's boundless energy. As she released me and stepped back, I asked, "And why aren't you in school?"

Lucy planted her hands on her hips and said grandly, "It flooded."

"What?"

"It's true," Nick said. "A water line burst, and since it happened on a Sunday, no one knew until teachers started showing up this morning. They sent the kids home so they could get things fixed up."

Great. Am I conjuring waterfront property all over Nightmare now?

"How nice that you got a vacation day!" I told Lucy, trying to muster as much enthusiasm as I could.

"It's not a vacation," Lucy and Nick chorused. She sighed dramatically. "I have to go finish my homework." Lucy turned and stomped with her pink sneakers to a folding chair at one side of the bay. She opened a textbook with a flourish and held it up in front of her face.

"Nick, you know a lot of folks in this town," I said. "What can you tell me about the town psychic?"

"Alana Unger is a hack," Nick said with a sniff. "I don't know how she stays in business. I guess enough of the tourists go there, since they don't know any better. Mia went to her once. It was for a bachelorette party, of all things. Alana told Mia she would be dead in eighteen months. Shows what she knows."

Lucy lowered the book. "But Mom did die, remember?"

CHAPTER ELEVEN

I gasped and pressed a hand to my chest. "What? Wait, no, that's not right. Lucy, your mom is still alive. I just saw her last week!"

Lucy giggled and made a face that clearly said I was being ridiculous. "She's not dead anymore!"

I looked at Nick for a translation. "Lucy's technically correct," he said. "Six months after the bachelorette party, Mia was renovating Lucy's bedroom, converting it to pink everything. She forgot to cut the power to the light fixture before trying to remove it. The shock stopped her heart briefly."

"We were there when it happened," Lucy said. "She wasn't breathing at first, and then she went..." Lucy opened her mouth in a wide *O* and inhaled loudly. "You know what's weird, though? Before that, I thought I saw her standing in the corner of the room, even though she was dead on the floor. It was like I had two moms!"

Nick continued as if he hadn't heard what Lucy had just said. "I don't think it counts as dying. Like I said, Alana is full of it with her death predictions."

I wanted to argue that Mia had, in fact, died, if what Lucy was saying was correct. She had seen her mother's spirit in those brief moments before Mia's heart and lungs kicked into gear again. "How old were you when that happened, Lucy?" I asked.

Lucy raised her arm, the fingers of her hand splayed. She had seen the ghost of her own mother when she was just five years old. I wanted to ask her more questions, especially since I knew Lucy had also spotted a ghost on the playground at school a couple of times, but I wasn't sure how Nick would react to the topic.

"Why do you need a psychic, anyway?" Nick asked casually, leaning over the engine of the truck again.

I laughed. "I don't! The guy who was just"—I glanced at Lucy, and even though she seemed to have returned to her book, I changed tack—"the guy who's room flooded at the motel apparently visited her, and he was raving about how she was a fake."

"According to my mom, that wasn't the only thing he was raving about." Nick's voice echoed from the bowels of the truck.

I was on the verge of telling Nick I thought Leonard had been right to accuse Sammy of stealing when I heard the sound of a car pulling into the parking lot. I turned and saw a gray sedan coming to a stop near the door of Nick's office area.

I recognized the car, and by the time Clara had climbed out of the driver's seat, I was laughing. "Fancy meeting you here!" I called.

"Olivia! Is it oil change day for everyone at the Sanctuary?" Clara walked toward me, adjusting the bright-blue knit cap that was pulled down over her fairy ears. The hat and her dark sunglasses made her look like a celebrity trying to avoid the paparazzi.

"I just stopped by for a chat with Nick," I clarified.

Nick lifted his head again from the engine. "Hello, ma'am. Be right with you!"

"While you wait," I said, "can you tell me anything about Alana, the town psychic?"

Clara looked surprised. "No. I've never met her. If you want a reading, I'm sure Vivian would be more than happy to do it."

I put a hand against Clara's elbow and gently steered her away from Nick and Lucy. I lowered my voice and said, "Leonard, the man who was murdered at the motel, was raving about what a fake Alana is just a couple days before he was killed. Vivian already told us about the conversation she had with him, and I'm hoping Alana will open up, too. She might know something that will help us find his killer."

Clara reached up and pulled her sunglasses down, just enough so she could peer at me with her violet eyes. "Why do you need to talk to her? Shouldn't the police do it?"

"It was Damien's idea," I said, slightly defensively. "Not to talk to Alana, but to find Leonard's killer. I'm trying to prove his death had nothing to do with me and my conjuring skills."

Clara laughed loudly, a musical sound that carried all the way to Lucy, who dropped her book in her lap and stared curiously at Clara. "Olivia, please! Of course you didn't conjure his death. A conjurer can move heaven and earth, but their desire has to be intense and unblemished. You're not the type to truly wish for someone to die."

"But I wished for him to leave Nightmare so he wouldn't keep all of us up at night with his shouting."

Clara put a hand on each of my shoulders and squeezed. "Trust me, you didn't bring this about. I know Damien is convinced you're a conjuror, and I think he's probably right, but you aren't a villain." Clara released me and raised a finger. "But, if it makes you feel better to solve this murder, then I'll help however I can."

"Thanks, Clara."

"Your name is Clara?"

I looked down to see Lucy had walked over to us. She was still staring at Clara, a slightly dazed expression on her face.

"Yes. And who are you?"

"I'm Lucy Dalton." Lucy pointed toward Nick. "He's my dad, and my grandma and grandpa own the motel where Miss Olivia lives. What were you saying about a murder?"

"Nothing, Lucy. Don't you worry about it," I said quickly.

Lucy's face fell. "Oh. Okay. I thought maybe you were talking about that man who got shot at the motel."

I put my face in my hands and snorted out a laugh. Of course Lucy had heard the news already. The way gossip flew through Nightmare, the kids had probably been talking about nothing else when they got to school that morning, right before they went home because of the broken pipe.

Clara leaned down so she was face-to-face with Lucy. "You're very smart. Olivia is hoping to find the person who killed that nice man."

Lucy clicked her tongue and crossed her arms. "He wasn't nice. Everyone says so."

"It's not polite to speak ill of the dead," Clara said ominously. "I know a couple of ghosts, and they don't like it when people say mean things about them."

Lucy's eyes grew wide. "You know ghosts?"

"Sure. The next time you come to Nightmare Sanctuary, I'll introduce you to them." Clara pulled down her sunglasses again and winked at Lucy.

Lucy immediately turned and ran toward Nick, shouting, "Dad! Dad! Guess what? Miss Clara is going to introduce me to ghosts!"

Clara giggled. "Sorry. I couldn't help it," she told me.

"What a cute kid. Anyway, I just said I would help you, and I meant it. Are we going to talk to the town psychic now?"

"Oh! Sure! We can go while Nick is doing your oil change." I had planned to chat with Vivian before visiting Alana, but Clara looked eager to go, and I figured there was no need to wait.

"We have to pick up Justine on the way," Clara noted. "If she misses out on this, we'll never hear the end of it." Clara was already heading toward my car, and as she went, she hollered to Nick, "The keys are in it. See you in a bit!"

I said a quick goodbye to Nick and Lucy, then followed Clara. As we drove, she had me tell her every detail about the murder. When I filled her in on what Tanner and McCrory had found at Sammy's, she shook her head. "He's already hidden that jewelry, I bet. If you did call in a tip, the police wouldn't find a thing. Your unexpected visit probably reminded Sammy that it isn't smart to leave stolen jewelry sitting out where even a ghost could see it."

Clara had a good point, and I really hoped I hadn't messed up the investigation with my visit to Sammy's office. I mulled that over while we looked for Justine at the Sanctuary. Eventually, we found her in the costuming room, rummaging through a plastic bin.

"We're going to see the town psychic, so Olivia can find a murderer!" Clara announced grandly after we said hello.

Justine looked at the bin, then back at us. "Gosh, here I was looking forward to an afternoon of cataloging hospital gowns."

I mentioned my desire to get the scoop about Alana from Vivian, but Justine assured me she and Amos would be fast asleep. "She sleeps more than most people, you know," Justine said casually. "Being so tuned in to the spirit world is hard work."

In short order, we were back in my car, and I found

myself repeating the details of Leonard's death all over again for Justine.

"Keep going," Justine said as I approached an intersection. "Route 23 is way on the south edge of town. Alana has been Nightmare's resident psychic reader for as long as I can remember. I don't think she'll appreciate us trooping in there and accusing her of being a fraud."

"I wasn't going to do that," I clarified. "I just want to ask her what she and Leonard discussed."

"Hear me out," Justine said. There was excitement in her tone. "I think we should go in as customers. We can each get a reading from her, and maybe, once we've buttered her up and paid her some money, we can ease in some questions about Leonard."

"I love that idea!" Clara enthused.

"I've never had a psychic reading," I admitted. "Okay, let's do it! Even if we don't learn anything, we'll at least have some fun!"

As it turned out, I didn't need Justine to point out where I was going. Alana's business was exactly as Sammy had described it. The low, one-story adobe building sat back from the road, looking slightly ramshackle. A green neon sign out front was in the shape of a hand, and inside it were the words *Palm and Tarot Readings. Know Your Future!*

I pulled into the narrow driveway and parked in one of the three spaces in front of the building. I assumed the other car there belonged to Alana herself, which meant we were the only customers.

Clara was practically skipping toward the door, and Justine had her hands clasped excitedly in front of her. I didn't share their enthusiasm, but I was amused by how much they were both looking forward to whatever we were in for.

When we reached the front door, I asked, "Do we just walk in or what?"

Justine pointed at a faded, handwritten sign taped to the door. "It says to knock." She was already making a fist to do that as the door opened.

The woman standing there didn't look anything like I had expected her to. In my mind, I had pictured someone who resembled the character Vivian played every night in the abandoned cabin vignette: lots of jewelry, a long dress, and a bright scarf tied around her head.

Instead of looking like a stereotypical mystic, Alana looked like a grandmother on her way to church. She was probably in her sixties, and her short gray hair was neatly styled. She wore a navy-blue skirt paired with a red-and-white-striped blouse. Rather than a stack of bangle bracelets, Alana was wearing a matronly pearl necklace.

I think Justine and Clara were as surprised by Alana's appearance as I was, because none of us spoke for a moment. Just as Justine began to say hello, Alana let out a piercing shriek and shrank back. "Death!" she screamed.

CHAPTER TWELVE

I clamped a hand over my mouth. I wasn't upset by Alana's pronouncement. Rather, her shouting about death the moment she saw us seemed to back up everything Nick had said, and I was trying really hard not to laugh. If I didn't act like I took Alana seriously, she probably wouldn't be all that cooperative when I started asking questions about Leonard.

Unlike me, Clara and Justine didn't seem to find anything funny about the situation. Justine was staring at Alana with a look of horror, and Clara had pressed both hands to her face. Unfortunately, their expressions only made the situation funnier to me. I shut my eyes and focused on calming myself down. *There's nothing funny about murder,* I told myself.

That did the trick, and I was able to lower my hand and say, "Which one of us is going to die?"

"None of you," Alana answered self-consciously. "Sorry if I scared you there. It's just that I realized you're here to talk about the murder at the motel."

Now it was my turn to be stunned. "How could you possibly know that?" I asked.

"I'm psychic," Alana said sarcastically, then she laughed. "Actually, I recognize you. You're the one who caught Jared Barker's killer. Luke Dawes was a client of mine, and you probably don't remember, but I was at his UFO watch party the same night you were."

"We were in a field in the middle of the night. I'm amazed you could see me."

"I've got good night vision," Alana said airily. "Come in, ladies."

I exchanged glances with Clara and Justine as we followed Alana inside. *So much for our cover story,* I thought.

The building was actually a house, and the living room was set up as a waiting area. There were dark curtains over the windows, so most of the light came from dim lamps sitting on low tables in the corners of the room. There was a plush but sagging couch along one wall, plus a few mismatched chairs. Wind chimes hanging from the ceiling tinkled in the breeze from an air-conditioning vent, and the room smelled of an earthy incense. While Alana herself didn't look anything like what I had expected, her business absolutely fit the bill.

"Sit," Alana said, gesturing toward the couch. "I'll be right back."

"That was wild!" Justine whispered as soon as Alana had disappeared through a door. "I thought she meant one of us was going to die!"

"Me, too!" Clara sat down and wrapped her hands around her knees. She had pulled off her sunglasses, and I wondered if Alana would be able to notice the color of Clara's eyes in the low lighting.

Alana reappeared a couple of minutes later, carrying a silver tray with three small teacups on it. They were made of a cream-colored ceramic, and they had no handles. "Green tea," Alana announced as she set the tray on the small coffee table in front of the couch. "Drink it, but leave just a bit of liquid. It will help me read the leaves for you." I started to protest that it wasn't necessary, but Alana raised a hand. "Just because you're here to talk about the murder doesn't mean you shouldn't get a glimpse into your own lives."

Justine and Clara eagerly reached for their cups, but I hesitated. Did I want to know what the tea leaves said about me? After all, I had possibly conjured a murder. I chided myself for even thinking that. Before I had started working at the Sanctuary, I hadn't even believed in psychics. I knew Vivian was legit, but by all accounts, Alana was just duping people out of their money. The only thing I had to worry about was that I would have a smaller cash pile until the next time I got paid, because I very much doubted this reading was on the house.

The tea was hot but not scalding, and I introduced myself between sips. I realized I needed a good reason to explain why I was looking into the murder, so I said, "I live at Cowboy's Corral, and the owners are good friends of mine. I'm eager to help them move past this as quickly as possible. I understand Leonard visited you after he arrived in Nightmare."

Alana sat down in the chair nearest us and folded her hands in her lap. "That man had demons," she said firmly. "He showed up here, saying he was afraid he was about to die, and he wanted to know if he would be safe in Nightmare. I read the cards for him, and I told him that he wasn't safe at all. He seemed to think being in the desert would protect him somehow, but the cards indicated he wouldn't find refuge here. He didn't like that answer one bit."

"What did he do?" Clara asked. She was leaning forward eagerly, hanging on every word.

"He started shouting at me and calling me a fake." Alana shrugged, and I got the impression it wasn't the first time that had happened to her. "People get upset when they don't hear what they want to hear, but it's not my job to lie to them. I finally got him out the door, after I threatened to call the police."

I had drunk all but the final sip of my tea, so I put the cup down on the tray. "Thank you," I said, even though Alana's story hadn't been helpful. "I appreciate you sharing."

"I'm not done yet, dear. That man came back here three more times, including a visit at one o'clock in the morning. This place is my home as well as my business, and I was fast asleep when he started banging on the door. He was screaming, begging for me to tell him the truth about his death. He said if I didn't think he was safe in the desert, then where else could he go to escape his fate? He was so desperate it was scary. I really thought he might hurt me if I didn't tell him a lie."

"Did you?"

"No. I didn't tell him a thing. Thankfully, by the time I had the phone in my hand so I could call the police, he got the message and left, though he kept shouting all the way to his car."

"Leonard really was worried about dying," Clara said. "How scary it must be to feel like you have a fate you can't alter."

Justine tilted her teacup and gazed down at the scattered tea leaves in the bottom. "I always thought being a seer would be awful. To know what's coming for people but unable to stop it must be frustrating."

Alana slapped her palms on her thighs and smiled. "There are good things to be seen, too. Let's find out what the tea tells us about each of you, shall we? Who wants to go first?"

Clara's hand shot up. "Ooh, me, please!"

"Right this way." Alana stood and gestured for Clara to follow her. The two of them disappeared through a doorway to our left. Instead of a door, though, there was just a heavy red curtain hanging in the space.

As soon as we were alone, Justine whispered to me, "Do you think Leonard knew someone was after him, and that prompted the prophetic dream he told Vivian about?"

"Maybe. That would mean someone followed him to Nightmare, though."

"I think you should take a closer look at the other motel guests, then."

"If I was staying at a motel, and I killed another guest, I would just check out the next day," I pointed out.

Justine raised an eyebrow. "Immediately drawing attention to yourself because you were so quick to flee the scene."

"Fair point."

Clara was sequestered with Alana for about five minutes. When she came out, she looked thoughtful, but she refused to say what Alana had divined from her teacup. "Later," was all she said as she sat down slowly.

Justine rose and grabbed her teacup. "I'll go next."

While she was gone, I tried hard not to stare at Clara. I wanted to know every detail of her reading, but her eyes were fixed on the wall ahead, and she looked like she was miles away. Whatever Alana had said had certainly given her food for thought.

A few minutes later, Justine emerged from behind the curtain with a smirk. As she returned to the couch, she motioned toward the room. "You're up, Olivia." Like Clara, she wouldn't divulge any details.

The reading room was small and even more dimly lit than the living room. The light fixture overhead had been covered in purple material, and it gave off an eerie glow. There was a dark jewel-toned rug covering most of the wooden floor, and a rickety round table sat in the middle of the room. There were only two chairs, positioned opposite each other, and Alana was seated at one. The cluster of candles on the table made shadows flick across her face as the flames danced. In the living room, Alana had looked like a stereotypical grandmother. In the reading room, she looked the part of the psychic.

"You brought your teacup?" Alana asked, extending her hand. I handed it to her, noticing that even her voice had changed slightly. It was slower and more breathy. Whether or not she was actually psychic, she at least knew how to set the scene.

I sat down as Alana gazed into the cup, tilting it first one way and then another. Every now and then, she would make little noises, like "hmm" or "ah." At one point, she put her nose close to the cup and sniffed. "A rose fades so quickly," she mused. By the time she set the cup down, I was gazing around the room, looking at the artwork on the walls. It was an assortment of paintings, mostly depicting old castles or cottages in dark forests.

"You see this?" Alana said, pointing into the teacup. I followed her finger and saw a line of tea leaves stuck to the side of the cup. I nodded, and she continued. "You've been in a long, dark tunnel, trying to find your way out. Don't worry. The light is coming soon."

I wondered if the tunnel was literal or figurative. Getting divorced, finding out my ex had spent every dime we had, and watching my friends run away from me because I was broke and struggling had certainly made me feel like I was in a long, dark metaphorical tunnel. Then again, Sonny's Folly Mine was an actual long, dark tunnel, albeit one with furniture and bedrooms.

Alana spun the cup slowly. She pointed to a small pile of tea leaves in the bottom of the cup. "I see a handsome man. He's in your arms."

For the second time since arriving at Alana's, I fought

the urge to burst out laughing. I bit my bottom lip, willing myself to keep a neutral expression.

Luckily, Alana wasn't looking at me. She moved the cup closer to the candles, tilting it toward the light. "He's crying," she continued. "Someone he loves is dead."

CHAPTER THIRTEEN

I bit my lip even harder. *Alana seems as fixated with death as Leonard was. Nick wasn't wrong about her.*

Even as I was trying not to laugh, I thought of Damien. He was easily the most handsome man I knew, though Theo ranked close to the top, as well. I tried to picture Damien in my arms, crying. *Right.* I was pretty sure the guy had never shed a tear in his life.

No wonder the people I had spoken to about Alana had insisted she was a fraud. She was also predictable. Even her statement about me being in a tunnel had probably been derived not from some kind of otherworldly insight but from the fact she already knew who I was because of her connection to Luke Dawes. She probably assumed that since I was new in Nightmare, I was trying to get a fresh start. In other words, I was trying to find my way out of a long, dark tunnel.

Sitting in that eerie room, with the candlelight throwing wild shadows and Alana speaking in an altered voice, I had started to believe, but my skepticism was back in full force.

Alana produced a wicker basket from somewhere underneath the table. It was about the size of a coffee pot, and she opened the hinged lid as she held it out toward me. "Pay what you feel this reading was worth to you," she said. "The suggested donation is twenty dollars."

I glanced inside the basket and saw a few twenties in there already. With a shrug, I fished my wallet out of my purse and added my own cash to the pile. If nothing else, it had been worth the money to hear about Alana's encounters with Leonard.

Since we had all gotten our readings, we said goodbye to Alana and left. As I drove toward the Sanctuary, I glanced over at Justine, who was in the passenger seat. "What did she tell you?" I asked. "You looked a bit smug when you came out."

Justine laughed. "She said I was a natural leader, though the army I command is made up of misfits."

Clara and I both joined in the laughter. Justine had taken over managing the Sanctuary after Baxter had gone missing. Even though Damien had arrived six months later to run his father's business, Justine had still remained in charge of much of the day-to-day operations.

"We are misfits," Clara said proudly.

"And what about you, Clara?" Justine asked, craning her neck to look into the back seat.

Clara was silent for a moment. "It wasn't so much what she said, but how she said it." In the rearview mirror, I could see Clara pull off her knit cap. She ran her fingers through her shimmering silvery hair, which spilled down around the pointed tips of her ears.

Justine and I remained silent, and eventually, Clara continued. "Growing up, it was always expected that I would join the family business."

"Clara's parents own Under the Undertaker's," Justine said to me. I knew the bar for supernatural creatures was run by fairies, but I hadn't realized they were Clara's family.

"I love my family," Clara continued, "but I didn't want

to work at a bar, and I certainly didn't want to work in a basement with no windows. I like sunshine and fresh air, and even at night, I like being able to step outside and see the stars. The idea of working at a bar from sundown to sunup made me feel…"

"Claustrophobic?" I supplied.

"Yes! I felt like I would just shrivel into a sad old lady if I had to be there every night. My family wasn't happy when I told them I didn't want to work with them, and I've always felt really bad about disappointing them. Still, once I started working at the Sanctuary, I knew I was in the right place for me."

"Your folks are nice enough, but I wouldn't want to be stuck in a basement all night, every night, either." Justine smiled. "You'd miss out on adventures like this, because you'd be sleeping off a long night of pouring drinks right now!"

"Exactly. So when Alana looked at my tea leaves, she said, 'You have two homes. Stay in the one where you can soar.' It was like she could sense the guilt I feel, and she was telling me to let it go."

"Oh, sweetheart," Justine said, reaching a hand back toward Clara.

"No wonder you looked so deep in thought after your reading," I said. "Clara, you have nothing to feel guilty about. I'm sure you love your family, and if they really love you, they'll support you doing what makes you happy."

I unexpectedly felt a lump in my throat as I said that. The people I had thought loved me most in Nashville really hadn't. They had loved an idealized me, the one with a big house, a nice car, and plenty of money. Here in Nightmare, people like Clara, Justine, and Mama supported the real me, the one who had arrived in town with no money, no home, and no idea what to do next.

By that time, I was pulling up in front of the Sanctuary

to drop off Justine. I put the car in park and turned so I could see both women. "I really appreciate your friendship."

Justine looked mildly surprised. "Of course. We're happy to help you solve a murder!"

"I don't mean just today. I mean all of it. You two have been great from the start."

"Not everyone in this world is a Damien," Justine said with a lopsided grin. "We're happy you've joined our army of misfits."

Justine already had the door open when she stopped and said, "Oh! What did Alana tell you?"

"That I'm in a long, dark tunnel right now, but the light at the end is coming." I didn't add the part about the handsome man crying in my arms. As preposterous as I found the scenario, it felt too personal to share for some reason.

"Maybe she meant the tunnels here," Clara said.

"I hadn't thought of that." There was a network of hallways that connected the various vignettes inside the haunt, so staff could get around without being seen. We referred to them as tunnels.

Clara moved to the front seat after Justine had gone inside. As we drove toward Nick's shop, I asked her for more details about Under the Undertaker's.

"My great-grandfather started it," Clara said. "When he realized how many supernatural creatures were coming here to work for Baxter, he saw it as a way to give them a safe place to go have some fun, but he also recognized it would make him a lot of money."

"Was your great-grandfather really old when he opened the bar? If Baxter was already here in Nightmare…" I was trying to do the math on Baxter's age.

"There's a photo of Great-grandpa and Baxter together in the forties," Clara said in a matter-of-fact tone.

"The nineteen forties?"

Clara giggled. "Yes, of course!"

"Was Baxter just a baby?"

"No, he was grown up. He looked a bit younger than he does now, er, than he did when we last saw him." Clara sighed. "I miss him. I hope he's okay and that I get to see him again."

"I hope so, too," I said. I meant it, but I was also still trying to wrap my head around what Clara was saying. "If Baxter was already an adult in the forties, then he must be incredibly old."

"None of us knows how old he is. And, of course, none of us knows *what* he really is. Baxter is one of the kindest, most generous people I've ever met, but he always refused to say what kind of supernatural creature he is."

"Surely you all have theories."

"Nothing seems to fit the bill. Vampires don't age, either, but Baxter eats food and goes out in the daytime, so he's not one of those. He's not gross enough to be a ghoul." Clara tapped her fingers on the armrest. "My best guess is warlock. I think he might have put a spell on himself for long life."

"Hmm. No wonder Damien is clueless about his own abilities."

"I kind of feel sorry for him. It couldn't have been easy growing up in Baxter's shadow. But even Damien doesn't know what his dad is? I would have thought Baxter had told him, at least."

"Nope." I hesitated, then added, "And Damien doesn't like to broadcast that he doesn't know what he is, or what his supernatural abilities are."

Clara mimed zipping her lips shut. A moment later, she groaned, her lips still clamped together. She raised her hand and made the same motion, but in the opposite direction, like she was unzipping her lips. "Aw, man, now

I'm feeling even more sorry for him. I swear, Olivia, if you make me start liking Damien…"

"I know exactly how you feel," I told her.

By the time we got back to Done Right Auto Repair, Clara's car had fresh oil in it, and Lucy had finished her homework. She had moved on to playing a video game on the small TV in Nick's office. I gave Clara, Lucy, and even Nick a big hug before I left. Between the tunnel talk and Clara's admission about her family, I was feeling especially appreciative for where I was and who was in my life at the moment.

I stopped in the front office after I got back to Cowboy's Corral. Mama was there, looking fairly calm. "You seem like you're doing better, but how are you, really?" I asked her.

"I'm dealing. I called the insurance company, and I have a to-do list for room twelve, so I feel less overwhelmed about the things that have to be done. But I'm still reeling that someone was murdered here."

"It's going to take time to process, I'm sure."

"Yes, but while I wait, I could use a beer! You want to go to the saloon with me tonight? Benny will be here around eight, so I can slip away for a bit."

"You're on!" Actually, I was pretty tired from a long day, but it was one of my nights off, and I knew Mama could really use the break. When I got back to my apartment, I sprawled on the bed and took an hour-long nap. The sun hadn't even set when I lay down, but by the time I got up, it was nearly dark out.

I opened the fridge to see what I could make for dinner, and that was when I realized I had skipped right past lunch. My stomach growled at me resentfully. I pulled out leftover spaghetti from the night before and dumped it unceremoniously into a pan. "You happy?" I asked my stomach as the smell of tomato sauce and garlic started to waft from the pan.

Once I was rested and had a full belly, I felt a lot more enthusiastic about going to the saloon. Mama had told me to meet her at the front office at eight, which gave me just enough time for a quick shower. I put on a purple dress that was maybe a little too short for a forty-two-year-old, but I didn't care what anyone thought of my wardrobe. With strappy brown sandals and a big, sparkly plastic ring I had found at a yard sale, I felt downright pretty.

Walking past Leonard's room, which still had the crime scene tape in front of it, brought my mood down a bit, but I felt better when I got to the office and saw Mama wearing a low-cut polka-dot blouse. She had added red lipstick that matched the dots to a tee.

We walked to the saloon, and since it was such a short walk, we were bellying up to the bar in less than ten minutes. For us, bellying up meant hopping up onto barstools that were just a hair too tall to be easy.

Mama and I had just gotten our beers when I felt a tap on my shoulder. I turned to see Tara Stokes, a server at the saloon. She was dressed in her usual saloon girl outfit, complete with a corset, a frilly skirt, and fishnet stockings.

"I hear you've got another murder on your hands," Tara said in greeting. She wasn't much for tact.

"Yeah, the victim was staying downstairs from my apartment at Cowboy's Corral."

Tara had a tray full of empty beer mugs balanced on the palm of one hand, and she deftly shifted it to the other hand so she could lean toward me. "I might have a little tidbit for you. He was in here the night he got killed. He was shouting to anyone who would listen about Alana. Do you know who she is?"

"The town psychic. We met earlier."

"He said that Alana had seen his death right here in Nightmare, and he could see hers."

CHAPTER FOURTEEN

"That sounds like Leonard wanted to kill Alana," Mama said.

"Do you think she heard about Leonard's rant, so she went on the offensive and killed him before he could kill her?" I put my beer mug down and brought my hands together in a gesture of gratitude. "Thank you, Tara. This is really interesting information."

Tara winked. "Happy to help."

"By the way, how is Miguel doing?" I just assumed he and Tara were dating again, since the last time I had seen them, they had been sitting closely together at a table there at the saloon. Unfortunately, that had been right before I had realized Miguel's mother had murdered his girlfriend, Kelly. Talk about complicated relationships.

"He's hanging in there. He goes to see his mom every week, even though she got transferred to the prison up in Tucson. I think he'll stop going so often before long, and then he can start getting on with his life here." Tara turned to go, but she stopped herself and said, "Thanks for asking. Half this town has been treating him like he's a criminal since all this happened."

"Hopefully, the dust will settle, and people will come to their senses. Miguel isn't a bad guy." Of course, I didn't add that I had once thought he was the murderer rather than his mother.

"He's a great guy. I'm lucky to have him." Tara smiled dreamily. "I've got to get back to it. Enjoy your drink!"

I waved as Tara bustled off.

"If you're writing up a list of suspects, there's one thing you need to factor in," Mama said without skipping a beat as soon as Tara had walked away.

"And that is?" I picked up my mug again and looked at her curiously.

"The security cameras."

Of course. I had totally forgotten the motel had two security cameras. One was pointed at the entrance to the parking lot, and the other was trained on the exit at the opposite side of the office building. Any cars coming or going—or any pedestrians, for that matter—would be on the footage.

"If we go by the number of cars entering and exiting the motel the night Leonard was killed, then just how many suspects are we talking about?" I asked.

"Zero. No one drove in or out of the parking lot that night." Mama took a big gulp of her beer, then wiped her mouth with the back of her hand. I noticed her cheeks had suddenly turned pink. "Except me," she added in a low voice.

"But you and Benny go home once the office closes for the night," I said, frowning.

"Yes, but I couldn't sleep that night. I didn't want to bother Benny with all of my tossing and turning, so I went for a drive. I made a lap of the parking lot while I was out, because I wanted to know if Leonard was shouting up a storm again. So, I pulled in, parked, and sat there with the windows down for a bit. I didn't hear a peep, so eventually, I left and kept driving until I was ready to give sleep another try."

"Why did you blush when you admitted your car is on the security footage? Are you worried the police will think you killed one of your own guests?"

"No, of course not. I just… I don't know. I realize it sounds weird that I was roaming Nightmare in the middle of the night."

"I don't think it's weird at all. I did a few late-night drives myself after Mark told me we were broke and he wanted a divorce." I plunked my beer mug down a little harder than I had intended. Just thinking about Mark and that whole situation used to make me furious. Now, it simply annoyed me. "After I had to sell my car and get the clunker I have now, I couldn't do that anymore. There was too big of a chance I'd break down somewhere."

Mama smiled and patted my arm. "Then you did break down, right here in Nightmare. I'm so glad you did."

"Me, too," I said, returning her smile. "Back to the security footage, though. If no one came in or out of the parking lot, does that mean another guest killed Leonard?"

"Or someone came in off the alley out back. You can't drive that way, but you can walk."

I knew that because I had walked Felipe back there when he and Mori had stayed with me for a few days. And if I knew that, then there were plenty of other people around town who probably knew about the alley access, too. "That means," I mused, "whoever killed Leonard probably knew about the security cameras. If they staked the place out at all, they would have spotted them."

"Exactly. Even someone from out of town could stroll past and see those cameras. Someone might have followed Leonard here and killed him."

"Which again points to Leonard being targeted by another motel guest," I added.

"On the other hand, it could have been a local.

Leonard might have had connections here in Nightmare that we don't know about."

I nodded. "And if that's the case, then those folks won't be popping into the police station to tell on themselves."

We both fell silent and lifted our glasses in tandem. The silence between us stretched as we both stared at our own reflections in the old mirror that ran behind the bar. I didn't know what Mama was thinking about, but I was thinking of Gabe, the neighbor who had seemed almost gleeful about Leonard's demise.

My well-dressed neighbor, Brian, would also be worth a second look.

And not just because he's handsome.

That thought gave me a start. Alana's prediction about a handsome man crying in my arms came back to me. In the moment, I had thought of Damien, but what if she had meant Brian? Suddenly, my brain was coming up with a whole new theory. Maybe Brian hadn't come to Nightmare to kill Leonard but to save him. Maybe they were friends, or real estate partners, or—

"Olivia!"

My shoulders jerked in surprise as I turned to Mama. "What's wrong?" I asked.

"Nothing, except I've been calling your name for half a minute. Your brain wasn't even in this zip code."

"I was coming up with wild theories, as usual," I admitted.

"I figured. But I was calling your name because you and I are both empty. You want another round?"

I looked down into my empty beer mug. "Sure. One more."

By the time we got back to the motel, I was feeling even more determined to talk to my neighbors the next day. First, though, I was looking forward to a long, uninterrupted night of sleep. Monday was my night off, and

Nightmare Sanctuary was closed on Tuesdays. I was only halfway through what counted as my weekend, so I curled up in bed without bothering to set an alarm.

I woke up Tuesday morning feeling refreshed. In fact, it was the best I had felt since I had discovered Leonard's body. The world seemed a little less dreary and scary as I sipped my coffee and enjoyed the sun pouring through the windows.

Once I was showered and dressed in jeans and a white T-shirt, I marched up to the office. Benny was the one behind the counter, and as soon as he saw me, he grabbed a piece of paper and held it out toward me. "Mama said you'd be needing this information, but if anyone asks, we don't know anything about it," he said, his gray eyes twinkling slyly.

The slip of paper had two numbers written on it. During our second beer the night before, I had told Mama how determined I was to speak to both Gabe and Brian, and I knew I was looking at their room numbers. I thanked Benny and headed to the closest room, which was just two doors over from Leonard's.

I knocked, half expecting no answer. It was nearly noon, so most guests would be out at that time of day, probably seeing the various tourist attractions around town. I was surprised, then, when the door opened, and I saw June standing there in black leggings and a pink crop top.

"Hi," I said awkwardly. "We met at the coffee shop the other day. Um, I wonder if you and your, uh…"

"Husband," June supplied, staring at me like I was an unwelcome door-to-door salesperson.

"Yes. The thing is, I'm trying to help the owners of Cowboy's Corral with this murder case, and I was wondering if I could have a little chat with you two?"

Gabe appeared behind June. His hair was sticking up

in every direction, and he was only wearing a pair of loose plaid pajama pants. "Do you think one of us killed him because he was too noisy?" he asked.

At first, I thought Gabe was joking. When I had seen him at The Caffeinated Cadaver, he had seemed jovial, and maybe even a little silly. As I looked at him, though, I realized he wasn't making a joke. He was glaring at me. My brain was saying, *Yes, I do think that's possible.* Instead, what I said was, "I'm hoping you might have seen something suspicious while you were shouting at Leonard the night before he was killed. Was anyone with him? Did you hear him mention someone?"

"We gave the police our statement, like everyone else here," June said firmly.

"I know, but—"

I didn't get to finish my sentence, because Gabe reached past June and slammed the door in my face. I wasn't even offended by the rudeness of it. Rather, in my mental list of suspects, Gabe's name was now in bold and underlined.

Still, I was disappointed that I hadn't actually learned anything useful from them. I looked at the second number on the paper Benny had given me, grit my teeth, and headed in that direction.

Brian was staying on the opposite side of the motel, so I cut through the parking lot. His room was upstairs, and I braced myself before I knocked on his door. I told myself to be polite but not to expect the same in return.

There was no answer, even after I knocked a second time. As I was turning away from the door, though, I realized the curtains over the window weren't closed all the way. I glanced quickly to my left and right to make sure I was alone, then I peered through the window.

I'm trying to solve a murder by looking through everyone's windows.

I hadn't garnered any clues by looking through the glass door at Sammy's office, but I whispered an excited "What?" as I surveyed what little I could see of Brian's room.

There was a green sweatshirt sitting at the foot of the bed. It was neatly folded, and it was positioned just right so I could see the design on the front with ease. It was the emblem for the University of Ohio, the same state Leonard had come from.

CHAPTER FIFTEEN

I didn't see anything else of note inside Brian's room, so I stepped back from the window and looked around again. There was still no one to be seen, so my spying had probably gone unnoticed. I walked slowly back to my apartment, pondering Brian's sweatshirt the whole way. Brian and Leonard just so happened to both be from Ohio. And they just so happened to have appeared in Nightmare, at nearly the same time, looking for real estate.

Just a coincidence, probably.

Coincidence. I was getting so tired of that word.

Because, maybe, it wasn't a coincidence. Maybe Brian and Leonard had known each other, and maybe Brian had figured into Leonard's death premonition somehow. I still wanted to have a conversation with Brian, but I was quickly forming a whole different list of questions I wanted to ask him.

I had been feeling so restless lately, but by the time I had opened up the laptop at my kitchen table, I was ready to get to work on my to-do list for the motel. Instead of feeling like a distraction, tackling some of the marketing projects I had in the works felt like a welcome escape. I got so caught up in finding the right adjectives to describe Cowboy's Corral that I was able to push rude guests and coincidental sweatshirts right out of my head.

I took a lunch break so I could scarf down a turkey sandwich, then got back to work. The Sanctuary was closed on Tuesdays, and it felt good to be getting work of a different kind done.

Then, at three o'clock, my phone rang. The caller ID told me it was Damien.

When I answered, he began, "Can you please work tonight? I need a fill-in for Justine."

I was instantly worried. "Justine? Is she okay? What happened?"

"Calm down, Olivia. She's fine. Or she will be, at least. She tripped on a piece of scenery in the cemetery vignette this morning, and she twisted her ankle. She needs to stay off it for a couple of days."

I relaxed and agreed to be there in time for the family meeting, but I added, "The Sanctuary is usually closed on Tuesdays. What's going on?"

"It's October, the one month a year we're open seven days a week." Damien paused. "You sound like you're on edge. Maybe we need to do some practice to get your emotions under control."

"My emotions are fine," I said tightly. Even as I said that, I realized they were not at all fine. I sighed. "Yup, I hear it, too. I'm not sure practice will do anything other than make me more tense and frustrated, though."

"What's going on that you feel that way?"

Damien and I didn't have the kind of relationship where we had heart-to-heart chats, so I started to brush off his question. I stopped halfway through the word "nothing," and suddenly, I was bringing him up to speed on what I knew—and how much I didn't know—about the murder. "So," I finished, "I'm worried one of my neighbors here at the motel is a murderer, and I'm concerned that this is all taking a big toll on Mama and Benny."

"Conjuring practice will be good for you," Damien

said confidently. "It might be the best way to keep your brain from going in a hundred different directions at once. How about we meet at five?"

"Sure."

"And," Damien said, suddenly sounding hesitant, "I think we should meet at the mine."

When I pressed Damien as to why we should practice there instead of at the Sanctuary, he would only say that it seemed like the right thing to do. At first, I thought there was something he wasn't telling me. Something he knew or had figured out but wanted to keep secret for some reason. As I continued to ask why we should meet at the mine, though, I realized even Damien himself didn't know the answer.

He just had a gut feeling. A vibe, like the kind Mama got about people.

"Of course! I have to ask Mama!" I said.

Damien snickered. "Do you need her permission to go out and play?"

"No, I mean I need to ask her about the neighbors. She reads people really well, and I had asked her about Leonard, but I should have asked her about the other guests, too. I have to go. I'll see you at five!" I hung up without giving Damien a chance to say anything else. I was too excited about what kind of insight Mama might have for me.

I slammed the laptop lid shut, put on my shoes, and hustled up to the office. Luckily, Mama was on duty rather than Benny. She was busy neatening the rack of brochures for all the tourist attractions, historic sites, and restaurants around Nightmare, and when I came dashing through the front door, she looked at me worriedly.

"Everything okay, Olivia?"

I stopped in my tracks and laughed self-consciously.

"Yeah. I've been a little high-strung today, but everything is fine."

Mama let out her breath in a loud exhale. "Good. One murder is all the bad news I can handle in a week."

"That's actually why I came up here. Mama, you get vibes from people, and they're usually accurate. Tell me about the guests who were staying here the night Leonard was killed. Specifically, I'd like to know your impressions of—"

"The Dennings and Mr. Wilcox," Mama finished for me.

I still had the slip of paper Benny had given me in the pocket of my jeans, so I pulled it out and held it up. "Exactly. The guests in rooms ten and forty-three."

"Your conversations with them must have been interesting."

"That's the problem." I reached out and grabbed a stack of brochures to help Mama. "Gabe slammed the door in my face, and Brian wasn't home. However, I could see a sweatshirt on his bed, and it was for the University of Ohio."

"When he checked in, I mentioned he wasn't the only Ohio resident staying here," Mama noted. "I joked that he and Leonard were my first snowbirds of the season."

"And did you get any kind of feeling from Brian when he checked in?"

"Honestly, my first impression of Mr. Wilcox was that he's one of the best-looking men I've ever seen. I almost asked him if he had stopped here by accident. People wearing clothes that expensive usually stay at The Nightmare Grand Hotel."

"He is awfully handsome," I agreed.

"On the outside, at any rate. In terms of the feeling he gave off, it wasn't impolite, but it wasn't friendly, either. I got the impression the man has zero sense of humor. He didn't even crack a smile at my snowbird joke."

"And what about Gabe and June?"

"Dishonest," Mama said immediately. Her lips tightened into a thin line. "The husband, especially. If we find out Mr. Denning makes his living as a pool shark or some kind of hustler like that, I won't be surprised in the slightest. There's something sneaky going on with him."

"And June?"

"She just struck me as a little impatient. Sorry I didn't get anything stronger that might help us find Leonard's killer."

"I figured I'd give it a shot, just in case. Thanks, Mama. I've got to get back to work on scheduling next week's social media posts for the motel. I thought I had all day to do it, but I have to fill in for someone at work tonight, and Damien—"

"Yes?" Mama drew the word out, her eyebrows waggling.

"He... I just..." *Oh, no.* I had almost let it slip that Damien and I were going to do conjuring practice together. How could I have been so careless? Mama didn't know the supernatural community even existed, let alone that I was a part of it. I cleared my throat to buy myself some time. Finally, I said, "Remember I mentioned a while back that we found out Damien's dad owns a mine on the edge of town? We're going to meet there before work. I've been eager to explore it some more."

Well, it's not a lie.

Mama's face brightened, and I didn't think her smile could have possibly gotten any bigger. "You two have fun."

I left the office with burning cheeks. When Damien had returned to Nightmare right on the heels of my arrival there, Mama had asked me to go easy on him. She seemed to think he had gotten the short end of the stick in life and deserved some compassion. She had also been eager for us to spend time together, and I had thought she wanted me to befriend Damien. Lately, though, it had become clear Mama had her hopes set on romance. I wanted to tell her I was kind of over men and relationships at the moment, thanks to my ex-husband, but I doubted it would matter.

When I arrived at the mine that afternoon, I was still feeling mildly embarrassed, as if Damien might take one look at me and know what Mama wanted for him and me. Instead of pulling the rusted metal door open, I knocked, buying myself a few extra seconds to pull myself together.

As I waited, I looked down at my feet and saw the rose Damien had told me about. I had said someone could have dropped it there by accident, but it had clearly been placed with purpose right at the foot of the door. The leaves were shriveled, and the red petals had turned dark, almost black.

I suddenly pictured Alana, her nose deep in my teacup, saying something about a rose fading quickly. Had she been referring to this rose? Damien had already mentioned it before I ever visited Alana, so she hadn't been seeing my future.

It's just a coincidence. Another one.

I was still staring at the rose when Damien opened the door of the mine, the old hinges squealing in protest.

"It's still there," I said, not even looking up.

"It seems disrespectful to just throw it away." Damien stepped back, and I finally looked up so I could walk inside.

The mine looked just as it had the last time I had been there, but being inside it still felt slightly shocking. It was jarring to see the hewn rock walls juxtaposed with the floral couch and brown leather chairs. The art hanging on the walls only added to the surreal scene.

Damien shut the door behind me, but it was still bright inside thanks to the sodium lights overhead. "Let's get started," he said. Clearly, he wasn't in the mood for small talk. That wasn't surprising, so I didn't bother being offended by his abruptness. I knew by now it was nothing personal.

"I assume I'm focusing on finding Baxter," I said as I sat down on the couch.

"I think you should focus on calming your emotions first." Damien perched on one of the chairs and looked hard at me. "You're still feeling frazzled by this murder."

"Yeah." I shut my eyes and took a deep breath. "And I'm not here to think about the murder. I'm here to think about finding Baxter." I'd had enough practice sessions with Damien that I knew focusing on one thing would help my brain slow down. I pictured Baxter as I'd seen him in photos: gray hair, a mischievous smile, and a suit that looked a couple of decades out of date.

I let my mind fill in the details, from the wrinkles on his face to the slightly frayed edges of his coat sleeves.

A voice boomed in my ears, seeming to come from every direction at once. "My ashes are my own."

I yelped and opened my eyes, looking frantically around the room. It had been a man speaking, but it had been less deep than Damien's voice.

Damien had half risen from his chair, one arm stretched toward me. "What happened?"

"Didn't you hear him?" I asked wildly. I stood, even though my knees were shaking, and began making a lap of the living room. "I think it was your dad's voice. It's the same phrase I heard coming from the mine the first night I walked past it. 'My ashes are my own.'"

"I didn't hear anything, Olivia. Only you heard it." Damien's voice was shaking, but I couldn't tell if it was from fear or excitement.

There was a strange feeling in my chest, like an invisible hand was gripping my heart. I felt slightly sick.

I turned to Damien. "I think it's time for you to say, 'I told you so.'"

CHAPTER SIXTEEN

To my utter amazement, Damien laughed heartily. "I told you so! You *are* a conjuror, and you just focused all of your attention on my dad so well that you actually heard his voice!"

I plopped back down onto the couch and pushed my index fingers against my temples. "I was picturing him in my head, Damien, and I thought how much I wanted to hear his voice again. Not only did I hear it, but it was the same phrase I'd heard before, when I passed by the mine months ago with Gunnar."

"Like I told you then, 'my ashes are my own' is a phrase he used to say sometimes. It was almost defensive. I remember one time, he and Malcolm were arguing over whether or not there should be an age limit for people to go into the haunt. Malcolm was really pushing to allow kids under ten, saying it would help because the Sanctuary was financially strapped at the time. My father got so mad at the way Malcolm was trying to force the decision on him, and he finally banged his fists on his desk and shouted that phrase."

"Did Malcolm know what it meant?" I asked.

"If he ever figured it out, he hasn't told anyone. As far as I know, it's as cryptic as most of my father's life."

I dropped my head until my forehead was resting on my knees. "I really am a conjuror. I actually did something supernatural." I could hear the disbelief in my own voice, but I couldn't deny the results I had just gotten. I should have been excited. Instead, I was simply stunned.

I felt Damien sit down next to me. "Again, let me say that I told you so." He laughed again, but this time, it was more self-satisfied.

Without looking up, I said, "Maybe I did conjure Leonard's murder."

"No," Damien said quickly. "You've been focusing on my father for months, and it's taken you this long to hear his voice again. You don't have the kind of power it would take to cause someone's death. Not yet."

Not yet. Those words sounded ominous, and I sat up and looked at Damien resolutely. "Then we need to keep practicing, because if I ever do have that kind of power, then I'm going to need to know how to control it."

That was what I did for the next hour. I pictured Baxter in minute detail, and I wished with all my might to hear his voice again, but nothing happened. "I guess I won't be an overnight success," I told Damien as we prepared to leave for the Sanctuary.

"You'll get the hang of it," Damien assured me. "Like you said, we'll keep practicing."

Since Justine was out for the evening with her ankle injury, Damien was the one who ran the family meeting that night. No one said a word when he walked up onto the small platform at one end of the dining room to address everyone, but I could almost feel the silent collective groan. Damien rarely had good news to share when he stepped up to the podium.

I heard a guttural noise from somewhere near my feet, and I peeked under the table to see Felipe curled up on the hem of Mori's gown. When he caught me looking at him, he snapped his jaws at me moodily. Even he seemed bothered by Damien's appearance.

"Are we getting another lecture?" Theo was sitting to my left, his zombie makeup looking more gruesome than usual. "Is daddy mad at us kids?"

Poor Damien. I opened my mouth to say something in his defense, but Damien himself beat me to it. The second he got behind the podium, he alleviated any fears by saying he was only there since Justine wasn't. He made a few announcements, then assigned roles to those of us who didn't have regular spots inside the haunt. I was, as usual, going to be tearing tickets up front.

Once we had been dismissed, Theo turned to me with mournful eyes, but his voice was dripping with sarcasm. "What a shame. I was really looking forward to getting into trouble."

"You pirates are all alike," I teased. "You think it's fun to break the rules."

"Oh, no, I followed all the rules when I was a pirate," Theo said earnestly. "If I didn't, I would have been locked in the brig. Or, worse, I would have been forced to walk the plank."

I giggled at the mental image. "Good thing saltwater doesn't kill a vampire."

"Daylight does, though. I never wanted to see the sunrise while treading water in the middle of the ocean."

Yikes. So much for our fun conversation.

Luckily, Theo seemed to realize he was straying into dark territory, because he suddenly smiled and said, "But now that I live here, I can break the rules as much as I like."

I put my hand on Theo's shoulder as I stood. "You're my favorite troublemaker."

Damien hadn't talked nearly as long as Justine

normally did, so I had plenty of time to chat with some of my other friends before I needed to get to my post at the front door. Felipe followed me as I made my way over to Seraphina's water tank on wheels. She had her elbows propped on the top edge, so her face was close to Fiona's. "You need to tell Olivia," Seraphina said firmly just as I walked up.

"Tell me what?" I asked, looking between the siren and the banshee.

Seraphina pushed a lock of her long golden hair behind one ear so I could clearly see her round, greenish face. "Fi has something she needs to tell you."

"It's irrelevant," Fiona answered in a husky voice. Her tone was a good sign. When she was upset, her voice would rise in pitch until it reached full banshee wail. She hugged herself tightly with arms that were nearly as pale as her long white gown. "But you're right, Sera, every bit of information helps in a murder investigation."

My ears perked up at that. "Do you know something that might relate to Leonard's murder?" I asked.

"I knew he was going to die," Fiona answered bluntly. "The night he was here, I was in the cemetery vignette, as usual. I had just made a teenager scream his head off when I got the flash."

I blinked at Fiona in confusion. "Like… Like a hot flash?" I asked. Even as I said it, I wondered if those were something banshees even had.

Seraphina laughed and splashed her silver tail in amusement.

"It's what I call the feeling I get when I know someone is going to die," Fiona clarified. "It was so strong that night. I ducked into the tunnels to note the time on a clock, and later, I found out my flash coincided with the man's arrival here. Banshees have a bad reputation because we're harbingers of death. But it's not like we choose who's going to die. We find out, then we go appear to that person or their loved ones. Our arrival lets them know it's time to set things in order and say their last goodbyes. We're just being helpful, but people are afraid of us."

"Since you're a banshee, it makes sense you knew Leonard was going to die," I said. So far, I didn't understand why Seraphina had been insisting that Fiona share this news with me.

"Here's the thing," Fiona said. "When I sense someone's death, it's always inevitable. Their life's trajectory is already set. I sense people dying from illness or falling in a terrible battle. I wouldn't sense something random and unexpected like, say, a fatal car accident. Leonard's murder wasn't a spur-of-the-moment thing. Someone was already planning to kill him by the time he showed up at the Sanctuary."

"Premeditated murder," I said. "Thank you. This is definitely helpful knowledge. Seraphina was right to encourage you to tell me."

"I was right," Seraphina said in a singsong voice. She blew an air kiss at Fiona.

When I got to my post at the front entrance, my attention was divided between the memory of Baxter's voice and the news that Leonard's death had been premeditated.

I wanted to solve Leonard's murder, and I wanted to find Baxter. There wasn't much I could do about either while I tore tickets and welcomed guests to the haunt. In fact, there was only one thing I could do, and that was practice my conjuring.

I focused my attention on the guests filing past me, and I wished that one of them would hand me some cash, telling me I was doing such a good job that I deserved a tip.

After half an hour of that, I finally gave up. Instead, I kept one eye on Zach, whom I could see framed in the ticket window. *I wish for you to be in a great mood. I wish for you to be happy and lighthearted.* I chanted those words in my mind like a mantra as I tore tickets and directed people to the bathrooms.

Finally, Zach paused between guests and shot a look at me. "What?" he growled.

I batted my eyelashes at him innocently. "What, what?"

"You've been staring at me for the past twenty minutes, like you're trying to beam a message to me telepathically. What do you want?"

So much for that. "I want you to be in a good mood!" I called. A few guests who could see the look on Zach's face laughed—they knew I wasn't going to get what I wanted. Zach just rolled his eyes and waved the next guest to the ticket window.

Damien came up behind me shortly before we closed for the night. "Can we practice some more tomorrow?" he asked.

"You mean can I practice while you watch and critique me?" I said it playfully, but just to make sure Damien knew I was teasing, I winked at him, too. "Sure."

I had a lot to think about as I drove home that night. It took me a long time to drift off once I was in bed, and the only reason my brain finally calmed down was because I did some practice on my own. I pictured Zach smiling and laughing, and I wished it really would happen.

When I woke up on Wednesday morning, I decided to make some food for Justine. If she was resting her ankle, then I figured she at least ought to have a home-cooked meal to enjoy. That meant I needed to go to the grocery store. I got dressed and strode out my front door with purpose.

Then I immediately froze, one foot hanging in the air on the way down to the first step. There was a police van and two police cars in the parking lot and, of all things, Sammy Simms's pickup truck.

I caught sight of Mama standing near a couple of police officers, and she didn't look upset, so I relaxed and made a beeline for her.

As soon as Mama saw me, she waved and called, "Olivia! Come here. You won't believe this!"

"What's going on?" I looked toward the open door of Leonard's room, but I couldn't see anything of note except a few officers standing in a huddle.

"Leonard's room flooded the night he was shot because the bathtub faucet was running," Mama reminded me. "The police turned off the faucet when they arrived, but they didn't pull the plug on the drain. They wanted to leave the room just as it was for the crime scene investigators."

"Is there something fishy about the bathwater?" I asked.

"This morning, we were finally given permission to start cleaning the room. Benny pulled the plug, but the water level barely changed. The drain was clogged. When he tried to clear it, he got a handful of gold necklaces and diamond jewelry!"

Mama got the exact reaction she had wanted out of me. My jaw dropped open as I stared at her. Just over Mama's shoulder, I spotted Brian Wilcox with the same expression. He was watching the police work, and clearly, he had been listening in on our conversation. He shook himself, then turned and hurried away in the direction of his room.

I also spotted Gabe in the small group of people who had gathered to watch the proceedings. I couldn't quite figure out his expression. If I had been forced to guess, I would have said he was nervous and hungover.

The news about the hidden jewelry brought up so

many questions. Had Leonard lied about Sammy stealing from him? Or had Sammy only stolen some of the heirloom jewelry, and Leonard had stuffed the rest down the drain for safekeeping?

And how in the world did this discovery tie in to Leonard's murder?

CHAPTER SEVENTEEN

I stayed outside Leonard's room until Gabe finally returned to the one he and June were staying in. I thought it was interesting that both of the guests on my suspect list were there to watch the police work. Again, I tried to remind myself that it was natural for them to be curious about the event, whether or not one of them was guilty.

It took slow, careful effort to back my car out of its spot because one of the police cars was parked so close to it, but eventually, I was on my way to the grocery store. I picked up ingredients for a taco pie, which was easy enough to make in my tiny kitchen.

By the time I got home, the police vehicles were gone, but Sammy Simms was still there. Or, rather, he had come back. His truck was parked on the opposite side of the motel this time, and I saw him standing at the door to Brian's room. I resisted the urge to go over and ask him more questions. Instead, I went inside and got to work on the taco pie. I had just pulled it out of the oven when my cell phone rang. A quick glance showed me it was Mama calling, so I stopped admiring the bubbly, browned cheddar cheese on top of the pie and answered the phone.

"I hate to ask you such a big favor when you have work tonight, but can you please watch Lucy for a while?" Mama sounded distracted, and her words came out like she was in a hurry. "Her mom has hair appointments at the salon until eight, and Nick had to run to the next town over to tow a car for someone. Benny tagged along with him, so Lucy is hanging out with me this afternoon."

"Of course I can help," I assured Mama. "But why can't you watch her?"

"The police just called and asked me to get to the station as quick as possible. I don't know what's going on, but it didn't sound like they had good news to share."

"I'm on my way to the office right now. I can watch Lucy up there and mind things for you."

Mama said a quick thanks and hung up, and by then, I was already reaching for my shoes.

I knew Mama was anxious to get to the police station when I got close to the office and saw she was already standing outside with the keys to her red vintage Mustang in her hand. She didn't even wait for me to reach her. Instead, she shouted across the parking lot, "Thank you, Olivia! I'll see you later!" She climbed into her car, and a few moments later, the engine rumbled to life.

Lucy was sitting in one of the sagging chairs in the lobby. Her feet didn't quite touch the ground, and she was swinging them back and forth. Usually, she had a sort of happy, adventurous energy, but in the moment, I could tell it was nervous energy.

I sat down in the chair next to Lucy's and put my arm around her shoulders. "You don't have anything to worry about," I said.

"She didn't feel right. Grandma. She was okay, but then she answered the phone, and it got darker"—Lucy raised her hands and bent her fingers—"like someone had turned out the lights, but only where she was standing."

"I don't think your grandma liked what she heard on the phone. You read all the little bits of information she was giving during that call: her facial expression, the way she was standing, the tone of her voice. Without realizing it, you picked up on all those tiny details and knew she was feeling bad."

"I guess." Lucy leaned her head onto my shoulder. "Is she going to be okay?"

"Yes. But she and your grandpa have been under a lot of stress because of this murder, so maybe you can do something nice for her. Do you want to make her something pretty while we wait for her to get back?"

Lucy straightened up, and I could feel the way she changed from nervous to excited. "Yes! I have construction paper and scissors and glue upstairs. I'll go get them!" She bolted out of the chair and dashed toward the staircase behind the front desk.

A few minutes later, Lucy clattered down the stairs, her craft supplies clutched in her arms. She sat in the chair behind the front desk so she would have a worktop, but not before I made her promise to let me answer the motel's phone if it rang. I wasn't sure how someone calling to reserve a room would react to a ten-year-old front desk clerk.

Damien and I had planned to meet at four o'clock for conjuring practice, and since we were well into the afternoon already, I called him to reschedule. When I explained why, Damien just said he'd come to me. Satisfied, I hung up and grabbed a magazine from the side table.

I was halfway through an article about the top ten tourist towns in Arizona—Nightmare was number three on the list—when I saw Lucy running toward me. When she reached me, she thrust out her arm, and I could see construction paper clutched in her fingers. "I made this for you!"

I gratefully took the paper out of her hand and realized Lucy had made me a rose with green and red construction paper. Immediately, I thought of the psychic's mention of a rose fading so quickly. "This rose will never fade," I said, half to myself.

"Nope, and it won't ever die," Lucy said proudly.

"It's beautiful, Lucy. Thank you." I gave her a big hug and promised I would put it on the front of my fridge the minute I got home.

Lucy returned to her perch at the desk, so I propped the paper rose against a brochure stand and returned to reading. I hadn't realized how much time had passed until Damien strode through the door. I looked at my watch, thinking he might have arrived early, but no, it was four o'clock on the nose.

"She's been gone a long time," I said under my breath as Damien walked over to me.

Lucy's head popped up from behind the counter. "Hello," she said. "You're Mister Damien."

"If you know who I am, then that means Olivia has been saying mean things about me," Damien answered. He crossed the space to the front counter in three strides and leaned across it. "And you must be Lucy."

Lucy looked slightly worried. "Has she been saying mean things about *me*?"

Damien threw me a sly look. "Actually, she said that you loved Nightmare Sanctuary the one time you got to visit. How would you like to come back for a backstage tour?"

Lucy jumped up and down, her eyes shining. "Yes, yes, yes, yes! Thank you, Mister Damien! I have to finish this art for Grandma while you and Miss Olivia plan my tour."

I raised my eyebrows at Damien when he returned to me. "You have a way with kids," I said. It was impossible to hide my surprise. Damien was a jerk to everyone, and I had just assumed that included kids.

Damien sounded slightly offended as he answered, "I'm not as much of a monster as you think I am."

I felt my cheeks flush. "I've never used that term about you."

"Let's get started."

I threw a glance in Lucy's direction. "She doesn't know about any of this," I whispered. "I don't want her to wonder what we're doing."

"In that case, focus on us being alone. You can sit quietly and wish for that, and she'll never know." Damien sat down next to me, pulled out his cell phone, and began scrolling through it.

I closed my eyes and started taking measured breaths. I pictured Nick coming back and whisking Lucy away.

I wouldn't say I fell asleep, but I was definitely well on my way to snoozing when the bell over the front door tinkled. I opened my eyes to see Benny and Nick both trying to squeeze through the door at the same time. It would have been funny if not for their worried expressions.

Damien and I both jumped to our feet, and Benny stopped short when he saw me. "She's not back yet?"

"No," I said.

"She hasn't answered her phone, so I guess she's in a pretty deep discussion down there at the police station." Benny started rearranging the flowers in a vase on the countertop.

"Is Grandma okay?" Lucy asked. She looked worried again, and she came around the counter to wrap her arms around her dad's waist.

"She's fine, honey," Nick assured her.

"Of course she is," Benny answered. "You and your daddy head on home, and I'll call as soon as she gets back. Now come give me a scratchy kiss." He bent forward and opened his arms wide.

Lucy walked over and planted a big kiss on Benny's cheek, which was covered with white stubble. "It's so scratchy!" Lucy yelled, giggling and wiping at her mouth. It was clearly a little ritual the two of them shared.

After Lucy hugged me, she boldly turned to Damien and opened her arms. "I'll see you at the haunted house!" she declared as Damien bent down to embrace her.

Leave it to Lucy Dalton to bring out Damien's soft side. It was adorable.

Once Nick and Lucy were gone, Benny kept moving around the lobby restlessly, neatening things that didn't need it. He took the perfectly straight stack of magazines and re-straightened them, then moved on to a succulent that was already in its rightful spot on a shelf. He slid the planter a few inches one way, then returned it to its original position.

"We're not alone," Damien commented to me under his breath.

"I was picturing Nick taking Lucy home," I whispered.

"That's a valuable lesson, then. What you focus on has to be very specific."

I nodded. "I should have pictured the lobby with only you and me in it."

Benny had moved on to the signs in the window, and as his fingers reached for the neon "vacancy" sign, I called his name. His arm froze in midair, and he said bashfully, "It's a nervous habit."

"So I see. Can we get you anything? Maybe a glass of water?"

"No, no, I just—oh! She's back! Sue is back!" Benny ran to the door, moving surprisingly fast for a man in his sixties, and threw it open. His look of relief quickly turned to one of trepidation. "Susie?"

Mama walked in slowly, looking deflated. And not just in the emotional sense. Her fluffy, wavy hair seemed to have flattened out, and it hung in limp gray strands around her pinched face. "I'm okay," she mumbled. She headed straight to a lobby chair and collapsed into it. Only then did she seem to notice Damien and me. "Oh, hell...o. Hello."

"Mama, what happened at the police station?" I asked as Benny stood in front of her and took both her hands in his.

"They say I'm a suspect." Mama laughed in disbelief. "My car is the only one on the security cameras from that night, and I told them I couldn't sleep and went for a drive, but they think I might have come here just to...just to..."

"But of course you didn't," Benny said. "If the police really believed you killed Leonard, they would have arrested you."

"Besides," I said, "you even told me about your late-night drive. If the police can verify the motel wasn't your only stop, they'll see you were just out cruising. Did you give them your route so they can look for you on traffic cameras?"

Mama laughed again, and it had a hysterical edge to it. "Nightmare doesn't have traffic cams. We don't even have traffic! Besides, I can't tell the police where I went. Not ever."

Benny and I exchanged a glance over Mama's head. He looked grim, while I just felt confused. Mama shifted in her chair, crossing her legs and turning her head away from all of us. "You're right, Benny," she said. "The police don't really think I did it. They're just following every lead they can find, and my Mustang was a big red flag. I have nothing to worry about. I hope."

Benny was looking down at Mama with a sad, sympa-thetic expression. "Susie, it's time."

Mama shook her head wildly, but she kept her face turned away from us. "No! I promised I would never tell."

Benny crouched down and looked at Mama until she

finally, reluctantly, met his eyes. "He needs to know," he said softly.

I saw a tear slide down Mama's cheek as she turned and looked up at Damien. "I'm so sorry. Your daddy made me promise never to tell. But Benny is right. It's time you knew the truth. Damien, honey, your mama was my sister. I'm your aunt."

CHAPTER EIGHTEEN

I pressed both hands over my mouth and turned to look at Damien. The color drained out of his face, and he stared at Mama with unblinking eyes. When he finally spoke, it was so quiet I could barely hear him. "What?" he breathed.

Mama stood and started to reach toward Damien, then hesitated. "Baxter made me promise not to tell," she said. "He was afraid you would start asking me questions about your mother."

Damien's head shook just barely. "Why shouldn't I ask questions about her?"

"She was the best sister ever, and an incredibly gifted psychic, but as she got older, her power grew, and she couldn't control it. If she got upset, her emotions could unleash her psychic power. Anyone on the receiving end of that…"

Mama stopped and cleared her throat, then continued, "Baxter knew that if you were even half as powerful as Lucille, you'd be dangerous, too. He decided when you were just a baby that he would teach you to push down your abilities the second you started to display them. And he made me promise not to say anything, because he thought if you didn't know anything about her, then you would never *be* like her."

Damien swallowed hard. I had no idea what he was feeling. He was still staring at Mama, but his expression was slack. "What happened to her?" he asked evenly.

Mama waved a hand. "Your guess is as good as mine. It's like she just ceased to exist. There was no warning, no body, nothing. One day, she was there, and the next, she wasn't. By that time, she was living in the mine. It was warded to contain her power, and the door was locked from the inside the day she disappeared."

So not only did Baxter disappear, but so did Damien's mother. I instinctively reached out and took Damien's hand. His fingers were limp in mine, and I knew he was in shock.

Mama sniffed and wiped her damp cheeks with her fingers. "That's where I went the night Leonard was murdered. After I had stopped by here to make sure he wasn't raising a ruckus, I went to the mine. I hadn't thought about it for years, but ever since you mentioned it, Olivia, I haven't been able to get it out of my head."

I gasped. "The rose! You're the one who put it there!"

"I clipped it from my rosebush before I went for my drive."

"My father was holding my mother prisoner?" Damien asked. There was still no emotion in his voice, and I got a bad feeling that, at some point, he wouldn't be able to hold it all in anymore. I worried Damien would get angry, toward both Mama and his father.

And that, of course, could unleash whatever dangerous power Damien might possess.

"She wasn't a prisoner," Mama said. "Lucille was frightened by her own power. She knew her potential for destruction. She picked out all the furniture in that mine, and she moved in with plans of never leaving it. She wasn't alone, though. Baxter was with her, and you were, too, Damien. For a short time, at least. You were born there."

Damien's fingers twitched under mine, and I gave them a squeeze. I couldn't imagine how he was feeling.

Mama gestured toward me. "I nearly fell out of my chair when you waltzed in here one day wearing her necklace."

My free hand strayed up to the silver chain around my neck and the two delicate pendants that hung from it. One was a cross, and the other was a pentagram. Damien had told me the necklace had been a gift from his dad to his mom, and that there were powerful protection spells on it. Damien had given it to me to keep me safe.

Mama smiled sadly. "It feels good to talk about it. I've kept all this bottled up for so long. I hated not being able to talk about Lucille."

"Other people in Nightmare must remember her, though," I pointed out. "Damien could have talked to any of them for answers."

"They wouldn't have had much to tell. Everyone thought Lucille was strange, even when she was just a teenager, and her marrying Baxter only confirmed their suspicions that she was the weirdest person in Nightmare. She had withdrawn from the world by the time she disappeared, and that was more than forty years ago. This town was eager to forget she had ever existed."

"I'm sorry you lost your sister," Damien said. "But at least this explains why you always seemed to have your eye on me while I was growing up."

Mama chuckled. "Like that time I caught you smoking behind the gas station and yelled at you? I had promised Baxter not to tell you I was his sister-in-law, but I never promised to leave you alone! It was easy to pretend I knew who you were simply because we live in a small town, where everyone knows everyone else."

No wonder Mama has been so eager for me to be nice to Damien and so happy when we spend time together. She wanted her nephew to feel accepted and cared for now that he was back in Nightmare. Suddenly, I was very, very conscious of the fact I was holding Damien's hand. I deftly slid my fingers away from his.

"Now that Damien knows the truth," Benny said, speaking for the first time since Mama had dropped her bombshell, "you can tell the police exactly where you were the night of the murder. They're all too young to remember your sister, so they won't turn the news into a scandal."

"Even if I do tell them where I went that night, I can't prove it," Mama pointed out.

"Still, telling them the truth versus refusing to say where you went will be helpful," Benny countered. "Like I said before, if the police really thought you did it, you wouldn't be standing here right now. But the more detail you give them, the more innocent you look."

"I'll go back there right now and get it over with." Mama looked at Damien again, and this time, she did reach out and put a hand on his shoulder. "I know it's a lot to take in. Let's talk when you've had a chance to process this news. Please believe me when I say I only ever tried to do what was best for you, and so did your dad."

Damien nodded but didn't say anything.

The phone rang as Mama was on her way out, and Benny hurried behind the counter to answer it. That seemed like the cue for Damien and me to leave. We walked outside, and I waved at the rear end of Mama's car as she peeled out onto the road. By the time I returned my attention to Damien, he was stalking away from me, heading for his silver Corvette.

"Damien, wait!" I called.

He didn't answer. He just kept walking. I wanted to chase after him, but I knew Damien wouldn't talk unless he wanted to. If he wanted to be alone, then I needed to honor that.

I was still reeling from the news when I got to work that night. I had arrived at the Sanctuary early because I wanted to check on Damien, and I wanted to deliver the taco pie to Justine. My first stop was Damien's office, but the door was locked, and there was no answer to my knocking. I was disappointed but not entirely surprised.

I trudged up the grand staircase in the entryway, heading to the apartments on the second floor. I ran into Gunnar as soon as I got to the landing. His sinewy wings were slightly extended, so he took up a lot of space. As I watched, he stretched his arms overhead, his chest flexing. He yawned loudly. "Olivia, did you make dinner?" Gunnar reached forward with a clawed hand.

I turned so the taco pie would be out of the gargoyle's reach. "It's for Justine. When you twist your ankle, I'll make something for you."

Gunnar laughed, a loud, booming noise. "Like I ever get injured! Good one!" Gunnar smacked a hand against his broad, bare chest. His gray skin resembled stone that was covered in a greenish moss, and I expected it was as strong as stone, too.

"Where is her place, anyway?" I tried not to stare at Gunnar. Between his muscular physique and the fact he wore no clothing, I had a difficult time doing it. Before working at the Sanctuary, I had thought gargoyles were just ugly little statues that decorated churches. Not only were gargoyles real, but Gunnar proved they could be kind of hot, too.

Gunnar turned sideways so he could point. "Second hall on the left, third door on your right."

"Thanks!" I slipped past Gunnar and followed his directions.

Many of the Sanctuary's supernatural creatures both

lived and worked there. The second floor, which had once been hospital rooms, had been renovated into apartments. When I knocked on Justine's door, she called for me to come in, and I found her sitting on a love seat with her foot up on an ottoman.

She thanked me for the taco pie when I set it on the table beside the love seat, then she held her hand in the direction of a doorway. "Watch out," she said. I stepped back instinctively, and a moment later, a fork flew into her hand. "Madge did my dishes for me earlier, and I asked her to leave it all out on the countertop. That way, I can just grab whatever I need without getting up."

I grinned. "I guess telekinesis does help when you're laid up with a bad ankle."

"Seriously, how do regular people get by?" Justine winked at me, then asked for the latest in the murder investigation. I gave her a bare bones update before I headed out for that night's family meeting.

I had expected Damien to be running the show again, but instead, it was Clara. Damien's office was still locked up tight right before the Sanctuary opened for the night. I tried again on my break, but there was still no sign of Damien. Before I had to get back to my post at the front entrance, I dashed out to the parking lot. His car was nowhere to be seen.

If Damien wasn't at the Sanctuary, then he was probably at the mine. I was so antsy the rest of the night that Zach asked me if I had chili powder down my jeans. The second the Sanctuary closed for the night, I grabbed my purse from my locker in the staff bathroom and dashed for my car.

As I had suspected, Damien's Corvette was parked outside the mine. I pulled over behind his car and hurried to the front door. I knocked, but even as I did, I was yanking it open. "Damien?" I called.

The overhead lights were off, but there were a few lit candles illuminating what we called the living room, which was the front and widest part of the old mine. I could see Damien sitting on the couch, bent forward with his head in his hands.

Damien stood quickly, coming around the couch so we were standing face-to-face. "What are you doing here?" he growled.

"I came to see if you're okay." I was suddenly doubting my decision. Should I have given Damien his privacy?

"That was stupid."

Oh, I definitely should have left him alone.

Damien hitched in a breath and continued, "Of course I'm not okay." His voice cracked on the last word.

Without hesitation, I reached out and pulled Damien to me. His arms slid around my waist, and he buried his face in my shoulder. His body heaved as he started to cry.

I hugged Damien tightly and rubbed his back.

She was right, I thought. *The town psychic was right.*

CHAPTER NINETEEN

I had no idea what to say to Damien that might make him feel better, so I just stood there and held him as tightly as I could until he began to grow calm. Finally, he took a shuddering breath and lifted his head.

"It's late, and we've both had a long day. We should go," he said. His throat sounded raw. "Thank you."

"You're welcome."

Damien silently blew out the candles, and neither one of us spoke again until we were standing outside the mine.

"Call me if you need anything," I said.

Damien nodded once and headed for his car.

As exhausted as I was, I had a hard time falling asleep that night. Between Mama's news and the fact Alana's vision of a handsome man crying in my arms had been right on the money, I was feeling overwhelmed. When I woke up on Thursday morning, there was a part of me that wanted to stay in bed, where I could hide away from the world and let everything sink in.

There was another part of me that wanted to do the right thing. So, after a quick shower, I put my coffee in my travel mug and hauled myself up to the front office. Mama rose when she heard the bell above the door, and instead of looking happy to see me, she looked wary. "Are you mad at me?" she asked.

I was taken aback by the question. "Why in the world would I be mad at you?"

"Because I hid the truth from Damien."

I walked over and plunked my mug down on the counter. "You were only doing what Baxter had asked you to do, because he was trying to keep his son safe."

"Yes, but it made life hard for Damien, never knowing what he was or what he was capable of. It confused him, and I couldn't blame him when he left Nightmare as soon as he graduated high school."

"That's on Baxter," I said firmly. "He could have told Damien the truth. He could have explained why he was making Damien push down his supernatural tendencies. I know everyone raves about how great Baxter is, but he's definitely lacking in the parenting department."

"None of us are perfect parents," Mama said, slightly defensively. "Losing Lucille nearly broke Baxter. He treated Damien the way he did because he was terrified of losing his only child, too."

"Lucy is named after her, isn't she?" I asked, the connection suddenly clicking.

Mama nodded. "Nick never knew his Aunt Lucille, and I've never told him much about her, but he knows I loved her a lot."

I wrapped my fingers around my coffee mug and leaned forward. "What was she like? What kind of psychic power did she have?"

The bell tinkled wildly at that moment, and I jerked upward. I looked over my shoulder and was surprised to see Brian Wilcox walking through the door. He was, again, dressed immaculately, this time in a plum-colored shirt paired with a charcoal-gray suit.

Mama immediately turned into the gracious hostess. "May I help you?" she asked sweetly.

"The water pressure is low in my sink."

"Oh! Is that why Sammy Simms was at your door yesterday?" I asked the question before I could stop myself.

Brian looked over at me curiously. "You're the one who keeps hanging around the crime scene."

I could say the same thing about you, buddy.

"I live right upstairs from Leonard's room," I answered. "I really can't avoid it."

"And no," Brian explained, "the plumber knocked on my door and said he was doing a routine check. The sink didn't start acting up until this morning."

"I'll send Benny around in about an hour to look at it," Mama promised.

That seemed to satisfy Brian, so he thanked Mama and left, still eyeballing me over his shoulder as he went out the door. As soon as he was gone, Mama said, "I don't send Sammy or anyone else around to do a routine plumbing check."

Mama obviously knew about the supernatural world since her own sister had been a part of it, but I didn't know if she realized just how big that community was in Nightmare. I didn't want to admit I'd been snooping around with the help of two ghosts, so I just said, "I think it's likely Sammy really did steal from Leonard. Remember, Leonard was convinced Sammy had taken his family jewelry."

"I still don't want to think the worst of Sammy. He's a good plumber." I wanted to point out that being good at unclogging toilets and snaking drains didn't automatically make someone a decent human being, but Mama wasn't done yet. "Put him on the list right along with Brian. I said I hadn't gotten a vibe from him, but something is clearly going on."

"They're both on my suspect list already." I chatted with Mama for a few more minutes, then left to do something my old self—the one who thought the idea of real ghosts and vampires was ridiculous—would have laughed at: I was going to consult a psychic.

I pulled up in front of Alana's business feeling slightly silly, so there probably was a part of me that still held on to the skepticism of Old Olivia. Plus, there was the fact everyone I spoke to was convinced Alana was a fake. There was a car parked outside Alana's already, so instead of going in, I sat in my car and waited. In about ten minutes, an elderly woman shuffled out the door. Once she was gone, I went to the front door and rang the bell.

This time, Alana didn't shout "death" when she opened the door. Instead, she just smiled, like she had been expecting me.

"The things you saw in my tea leaves have come true," I said. "You're known around Nightmare for predicting death, but how good are you at solving murders?"

Alana's lips formed a thin line, and she crossed her arms. "I know some police departments work with psychics, but the officers here are a bit skeptical. Most of them, at any rate."

"It's not the police asking for your help, though," I pleaded. "It's me."

Alana looked me up and down, then sighed and waved me inside. She led the way to the living room, taking a seat in one of the chairs while I settled onto the couch. "How can I help?" she asked.

"Anything you can tell me about Leonard's visits here could be helpful," I prompted.

Alana's eyes got an unfocused look, and I figured she was searching her memory. "No," she said slowly, "I don't believe I left anything out when we spoke before. He was so horrible to me, but I think it was driven by his panic."

"Did he happen to mention Sammy Simms?"

"The plumber?" Alana's eyes snapped back into focus as she looked at me in confusion.

"Leonard had accused Sammy of stealing from him."

Alana shook her head. "Leonard only talked about the vision of his death, not crime. He was solely focused on how he could keep from dying."

I tried asking a few more pointed questions, but I got nowhere. It seemed Leonard had been desperate for answers about how to avoid his death, so he hadn't mentioned any names or anything personal. It had all been about staying alive. I realized Alana didn't have anything that could help me pin down a suspect, so I thanked her and left, but not before she produced her basket and waved it toward me with a sly smile. I grudgingly put a twenty in it.

It was past lunchtime by then, and I was starving. The smart thing, especially after having to pay the psychic for zero information, would have been to eat at home, but instead, I drove to The Lusty Lunch Counter. I needed comfort food, and for me, that was a cheeseburger and fries.

When I walked into the diner, I immediately started laughing. Emmett was perched on one of the stools. I plopped down onto the empty stool to his right and said, "We have to stop meeting like this."

"I was a regular here before you were," Emmett pointed out.

Ella slid a diet soda across the stainless steel surface. "Hey, Olivia. Have you solved that murder at the motel yet?"

"Not yet."

"Maybe a cheeseburger will help you put the pieces together."

As Ella moved away to put in my usual order, Emmet tilted his head toward me. "You're not harassing my new client, are you?"

"Brian? Not at all. How's it going with his search for an investment property?"

"Good, good." Emmett sat up a little straighter and brought his palms together. "He's looking at a great old house on Route 23 that would make a fantastic B and B. Two stories, about a century old. You might have noticed it because it's right next door to the town psychic, and there's no missing her place."

I sucked in my breath so fast that I started to choke on the sip of soda I had just taken. Emmett thumped my back as I coughed. When I had recovered, I said, "Sorry. It went down the wrong pipe."

I found it interesting Brian was eyeing a property right next to the very place Leonard had been going. There seemed to be so many little threads in this case, but none of them made any real connections. There were plenty of coincidences, but few solid leads.

It took me twice as long as usual to eat my cheese-burger and fries, because I was so busy thinking. I kept pausing mid-chew to consider the possibilities. Once, Ella came to check on me when I had frozen with my burger halfway to my mouth.

I was still going over what I knew about Leonard when I arrived at the Sanctuary for work that night. Justine was back on her feet, and I knew everyone was happy that she was leading the family meeting again, and Damien was nowhere in sight. I seemed to be the only person who really wanted to see Damien, and as soon as the meeting was done, I dashed to his office. I was going to be in the lagoon vignette that night, and before I changed into my pirate costume, I wanted to check on him.

Half of me expected his office door would be locked up tight again, but instead, it was standing wide open. Damien was sitting behind his huge desk, and his chin was tilted down so he could read a stack of papers that were in front of him.

"Hey," I called softly. "How are you doing?"

Damien barely looked up. "Fine."

"You want to talk?"

"No."

"Do you want to start practicing?"

That, at least, got Damien to look at me. "The haunt opens in less than half an hour. If you want to practice, we can do it tomorrow."

"I didn't mean me. I meant, now that you know more about your mom and what she was, you have a good starting point to figure out what you're capable of. I'm willing to help *you* practice."

Damien had picked up the paper on top of the stack, and it crumpled as his fingers curled around it. "No."

"Why not? You said I could be dangerous if I didn't practice, and the same could be true of you."

Damien's eyes flashed with a green light as he glared at me. "I understand now why my father taught me to bury my abilities. I'm not supernatural. I'm a monster."

"Oh, Damien, don't think like that." I moved around his desk and reached toward him, right as I heard someone clearing their throat from the doorway. I looked up and saw Zach standing there, his eyes gazing everywhere but at Damien and me. *How much did he hear?*

"You have a visitor," Zach said stiffly.

"I don't want to see anyone," Damien snapped.

"Not you. It's a visitor for Olivia."

Zach leaned back so he could look into the hall, and he waved an arm. A moment later, Alana appeared next to him. She kept her eyes locked on mine as she walked into the room. "I've seen another death," she said, her voice at a dramatic pitch. "It's yours."

CHAPTER TWENTY

"Oh, please," Zach said. His chest bowed out under his tight black Sanctuary T-shirt. "You told me you were here to help Olivia. Come on, I'll show you out."

"Zach, wait," I said. To Alana, I asked, "What did you see?"

"The spirits showed me an image in my mind. You were in bed, and at first, you thought it was a dream. But you felt the knife go through your heart and knew it was real." Alana's voice shook.

"Did you see who did it?"

"It was a man, and he was wearing an expensive watch. I couldn't see his face, but I could sense that you recognized him. There's a man you know who isn't so nice, even if you think otherwise."

"If I was asleep in bed, does that mean he broke into my apartment to kill me?" My heart felt like it was going to thump right out of my chest.

"I have told you all that I saw." Alana's hand twitched, and for a wild moment, I thought she was going to ask me to give her cash. Instead, she raised her arm, and her fingers curled around her pearl necklace.

She's literally clutching her pearls. If I hadn't been worried my death was imminent, I would have found it funny.

Just as Alana turned to go, Vivian appeared in the doorway. "I sensed you were here," she said to Alana.

"Vivian," Alana said coolly. She brushed past Vivian and disappeared down the hallway.

"Somebody please explain what that was all about," Damien said.

"The *town psychic* paid you a visit," Vivian spat. She sneered in the direction Alana had gone.

"And she told me that someone is going to murder me in my sleep. A man wearing an expensive watch." I braced myself on the edge of the desk, feeling wobbly-kneed.

Vivian snorted. "And you actually believe her? Please."

"She gave me a reading when I spoke to her about her connection to Leonard. What she told me has come true."

"And that would be?" It wasn't Vivian asking but Zach.

I looked at Damien, who seemed to be as curious as Zach. I hadn't told him about Alana's prediction, so he had no idea it had been about him.

"I'd rather not say what happened," I told Vivian apologetically, even though I was still looking at Damien. "It was kind of personal."

Damien's eyebrows lowered ever so slightly, and I knew he'd be asking for details later. Me staring right at him was a dead giveaway that he had been involved in the prediction.

"Look," Vivian said, spreading her hands, "maybe Alana got lucky with her prediction for you. In a town as small as Nightmare, she probably knows who you are."

I nodded. "Yes, she recognized me."

"Then she likely knows a few things about you that she used to her advantage."

I thought back. *Is that possible?* Alana might have known I worked at the Sanctuary. She probably knew about Baxter's disappearance, and she might have known that his very handsome son was now running the place. It was possible Alana had made a lucky guess, I supposed, but how could she have predicted the crying part?

"Do you have a grudge against her because she's your competition in this town?" Zach asked. He was leaning against the doorframe, clearly enjoying himself.

"I can't stand her because I worked a Halloween carnival with her once," Vivian said. "We were both doing readings for people. I sat there and watched her tell a lady detail after detail about her late husband, but it was so obvious to me Alana was making smart inferences based on the lady's body language and the information she was giving up. The lady was convinced Alana was really communicating with the spirit of her husband, and she forked over a stack of cash." Vivian made a gagging noise. "So disgusting."

"Maybe she's both legit and a fraud," I said, still not willing to dismiss Alana's prediction. *Better safe than sorry*, I told myself. "She might really be a psychic, but one who only sometimes gets actual supernatural insight, so she fills in the blanks with her good guesses."

Vivian harrumphed. "I'm going to get settled into my vignette. Olivia, you have nothing to worry about. You're safe."

I wanted to point out that Vivian had also told Leonard he was safe, but I knew she already felt guilty about that. Instead, I gave her a small smile and told her to have a good night of scaring guests.

Zach trailed after Vivian, still looking delighted by the drama. As soon as it was just Damien and me in the room, I could feel the tension. "What did she predict?" he asked quietly.

I had known it was coming, but that didn't make it any less awkward. I really, really needed to work on my poker face.

"You and me in the mine last night," I said, my eyes

fixed on the bookcase. "Alana saw it, though she didn't know it was you. She just said 'a handsome man.'"

Damien gave a low laugh, and I felt the tension ease. "So you think I'm handsome?"

The bookcase was in danger of bursting into flames, I was staring at it so hard. "Sure." I tugged at the hem of my T-shirt, still not looking at Damien. "Okay, well, I need to get changed. We open soon."

I reached the doorway before Damien told me to wait. When I turned, he said simply, "I wear an expensive watch."

My eyes flicked to his left wrist. "Are you saying you might be the one who's going to kill me?" I had tried to say it jokingly, but instead, I sounded scared.

"I'm saying many people wear nice watches. I think Vivian is right. You're perfectly safe, because that woman was just making up something vague. Still, if you want to stay here at the Sanctuary tonight, you can. In fact, I think you should."

My brain immediately protested that it wasn't necessary, because I could take care of myself. In fact, a part of me still believed I had to take care of myself, because no one else would. I had trusted Mark with our finances, and look how that had turned out. I was still staring at Damien's gold watch, and I forced myself to meet his eyes.

He looks worried.

I nodded. "Thank you. I'll think about it."

"Where will you be working tonight? I'm going to set up a watch."

I narrowed my eyes. "Did you just make a pun about watches?"

"Not intentionally. And like you said, the haunt is about to open, so you need to get going. Just know that you'll be guarded tonight."

"I'll be in the lagoon vignette. I'll ask Theo and the others in there to keep an eye out, too."

I made a hasty exit, in part because I still needed to change into my pirate costume and do my makeup, and I had exactly seven minutes to do it all before the Sanctuary opened for the evening. I also left quickly because I was feeling... *What?* As I hustled toward the wardrobe room, I tried to figure out the strange sensation washing over me. I was definitely concerned about Alana's prediction, but there was something more. A strange feeling, like my heart wasn't keeping time, and my belly was doing loops.

I feel flustered. Admitting to Damien that I thought he was handsome had made me feel weirdly unsettled. It was more than my admission, though. It had also been the way he had looked at me when he offered me a guest room for the night. I was used to Damien's hard stare and his resentful attitude. I wasn't used to him looking like he cared. Especially about me.

"Oh, boy," I muttered. I had reached the wardrobe room, and I headed for the rack where my usual pirate costume hung. I grabbed it off the hanger and ran to a changing room, and soon, I was wearing my long red coat with lacy sleeves and the tall black boots that went with it. I stopped at the makeup table to plaster on bright-red lipstick, and I nearly poked myself in the eye in my haste to draw on thick eyeliner.

On my way out, I jammed my black tricorn hat on my head. There were double doors separating the east wing from the entryway, where stanchions and red velvet ropes had been set up for the queue of guests waiting to go inside the haunt. The doors were already closed, so I cracked one of them open and peered out. The first guests of the night had already filed in, nearly filling the room.

I retreated and went down a narrow hallway on my right. It led to a long, wide hallway that ran along the back of the building. It was how we all got between the haunt in the west wing of the building and the staff-only areas in the east wing. From that hallway, I could access the network of hidden paths that connected the vignettes. They allowed those of us who worked at the Sanctuary to get around without being seen by the guests.

We called the paths tunnels because they were so narrow and dark. It had taken me weeks to learn my way through them. As I walked, the lights overhead flashed three times, then went off entirely. That meant Nightmare Sanctuary Haunted House was officially open for business. When I reached the door that led into the lagoon vignette, I hurried through it and dashed up to Theo.

Quickly, I told him about Alana's prediction. "It could be nothing," I concluded, "but maybe not."

Theo leaned his face toward mine, and I could see the concern in his brown eyes, even in the dim light. "We'll keep you safe, Olivia. I'll tell the others to keep an eye on you, too."

The first guests of the night entered the lagoon vignette just a few minutes later. My brain was at war with itself, waffling between believing Alana's prediction and thinking the whole thing was ridiculous, as the guests walked across the low catwalk toward me. I took a deep breath, gave myself a shake in an effort to fling off the confusing thoughts, and focused on looking as menacing as possible.

As the night went on, I relaxed. I was having fun scaring guests, and every so often, Theo would circle toward me. Even Seraphina, who was submerged in a big glass-sided water tank at the base of what looked like a pirate ship, surfaced between guests to look in my direction.

I spent my short break munching on potato chips and chatting with Mori, who usually had the same break time as me. The first thing she said when she came into the dining room and saw me was, "I don't think you're going to die anytime soon."

I groaned. "Has word gotten out already?"

"Vivian mentioned this alleged prediction about your murder. Personally, I think the town psychic is just trying to get attention. And money. You went there with Justine and Clara, so she knows you're willing to open your wallet for her services, and she's going to keep finding reasons you need to come back to her."

I laughed, not because I thought it was funny but because I recognized the logic in Mori's words, and I realized that, maybe, I was merely gullible. "I bet you're absolutely right. She came down here tonight to scare me, so I'll scurry back to her tomorrow to learn more. You are awfully perceptive, Mori."

"I've learned a few things in my four hundred years." Mori sat down on the bench, the midnight-blue satin gown she was wearing rustling softly. We chatted until it was time for me to get back to the lagoon, and I went feeling light-hearted.

I thoroughly enjoyed myself after that, scaring one group of guests after another. At one point, a couple came toward me, and I recognized Gabe and June. Gabe was laughing, looking like he had when I had met him at the coffee shop rather than the glowering, disheveled version I had seen in his room.

Even with my costume on, Gabe recognized me as I stalked up to him, and he screamed dramatically in a high, thin voice. Then he laughed and put both hands up to his face, making an expression of mock fright.

In the dim light, I saw the gleam of an elegant gold watch on his wrist.

CHAPTER TWENTY-ONE

I instantly recoiled from Gabe. There wasn't a lot of light in the lagoon vignette, but it was enough to see that the gold watch he was wearing was an expensive one. I recognized the Rolex logo because I had seen it all the time on Mark's favorite watch. At least it had been his favorite, until he'd had to sell it for the money.

Gabe was still laughing as I saw movement behind him, and a dark shape loomed up. Malcolm's face appeared over Gabe's shoulder, and he leaned in to say something into Gabe's ear.

Gabe's expression of pretend fear instantly transformed into one of real fright. He let out a yelp as his body jerked in surprise. June seemed to find it hilarious. She clutched her stomach and bent forward, her eyes shut tight as she laughed.

Malcolm was standing close behind Gabe, and Gabe took it as his cue to keep walking. Malcolm stayed directly behind him, and soon, all of them had walked right out of the vignette. June threw a glance over her shoulder to give me a thumbs-up just before she disappeared through the doorway to the next scene. Clearly, she delighted in seeing someone get the better of Gabe.

I managed to wave at June, but my hands were shaking. Just when I had been ready to dismiss Alana's prediction about my murder as a way for her to get attention and money, one of the people on my suspect list had turned up wearing a nice watch.

"Hey, you good?" Theo said into my ear.

It was my turn to yelp. "Don't sneak up on me!" I snapped. I instantly felt bad, and I wrapped my fingers around Theo's wrist to keep him from walking away. "Sorry. That guy is staying at the motel, and he's wearing an expensive watch. I let myself get scared."

"I assume Malcolm is part of your security detail," Theo said. "He's been lurking in the shadows for the past two hours."

I laughed weakly. "Really? I hadn't even noticed him."

Theo grinned. "He's as good at sneaking up on people as I am!" To my surprise, Theo leaned toward me and planted a kiss on my cheek.

I wrinkled my nose. "Ew, pirate zombie kiss!" I made a show of wiping off my cheek.

Once the haunt closed for the night, the overhead lights blared to life, and I could see Malcolm standing near the back of the prop pirate ship. He was in a dark little angle between the ship and the rear wall, which was painted black, so it was no wonder I hadn't seen him.

I walked over to Malcolm and hugged him. It seemed to surprise him as much as Theo had surprised me with that kiss. He stiffened at first, then relaxed a bit and patted my back. "You looked frightened by that man, so I hastened his exit," Malcolm explained.

I filled Malcolm in on why Gabe's appearance had given me such a fright. Unlike Mori, Vivian, and Damien, though, Malcolm seemed to give credence to Alana's prediction.

"Maybe she is making it up," he said. "However, there's no harm in taking precautions. We'd love to have you for a sleepover."

I smirked at Malcolm. "Are we going to paint each other's fingernails?"

"Right after we put our hair in curlers." Malcolm lifted his top hat, showing off his bald head. He was so thin that without his hat, his head vaguely resembled a skull.

Once I had changed out of my pirate costume and was back in my usual jeans and Sanctuary T-shirt, I headed for Damien's office. The door was open, and Justine was in there. She twisted around in her chair when she heard me and said, "Speak of the devil! Damien was just filling me in on the gossip. Everyone has been talking about Alana showing up here to predict your murder, and I've been waiting all night to get details."

"Apparently, a man wearing an expensive watch is going to stab me in my bed," I said. I leaned forward and rested my elbows on the back of Justine's chair. "Which is why I'm taking up Damien's offer to sleep here tonight."

Justine craned her neck to look up at me, then she pointed at Damien. "He wears an expensive watch. Maybe you shouldn't stay here."

"I'm counting on Damien not to murder me, though I think it's crossed his mind once or twice."

"Ha, ha," Damien intoned. "I'll drive you home so you can pack an overnight bag."

Justine sprang up from the chair. "The Thursday night poker game starts at one o'clock sharp in the dining room, so hurry up if you want in!" She bustled off, and Damien and I followed her out of the office at a slower pace.

The drive to my apartment was a silent one. Damien seemed to be lost in thought, and I was still feeling a little flustered. Out of the corner of my eye, I could see him staring straight ahead, his jaw clenched.

Something had changed between us. I wasn't sure if it had happened at the mine, when he had cried about his mother, or if it had been happening for a few weeks. Since we had met, I had been happy to make Damien out as the villain in the story. Now, though, I was regarding him as an ally. A friend, even. And yet, there was some new barrier between us. I had seen the softer side of Damien, and he had quickly built up a wall so I couldn't get another peek at it.

Damien waited for me in the car while I ran upstairs to pack a few things. I didn't have a small suitcase or a duffel bag, so I grabbed a canvas tote bag and shoved pajamas and a fresh change of clothes into it. I took the bag into the bathroom and unceremoniously threw my toilet articles inside. In just a few minutes, I was back in the passenger seat of Damien's car.

As he began to drive us back to the Sanctuary, I told Damien about Gabe and June coming through the haunt. When I mentioned Gabe's Rolex, Damien said, "Like I said, there are a lot of nice watches in the world. If that psychic had told you a man wearing blue was going to murder you, then you'd be spotting blue shirts everywhere. Her prediction was too vague to be believable."

"You look nice tonight," I said pointedly. Damien was wearing a blue shirt under his black-and-white pinstripe suit.

In answer, Damien reached down and turned on the radio. We didn't speak again until we were inside the entry-way. I headed for the hallway that led to the dining room, figuring Justine could point me in the direction of the guest room I would be staying in. As I went, Damien called after me, "Meet me in my office in fifteen minutes. If you're staying with us tonight, you may as well practice before bed."

"Great," I mouthed as I kept walking. Since my back was to Damien, he couldn't see the pouty face I was making.

Justine was setting up for the poker game when I went

into the dining room, so Mori volunteered to show me where I'd be sleeping that night. She swept up the grand staircase gracefully while Felipe darted ahead of us, taking two stairs at a time. When I reached the top, he trotted to my side, briefly rearing up on his hind legs and pressing his front paws against my hip.

Mori led me down the entire length of the hallway, then turned into a narrow hallway on our right. She stopped at the second door on the left and opened it, then waved me inside.

I walked in, wondering what a guest room at a haunted house attraction full of supernatural creatures would even look like, and found myself utterly astonished. I had expected something slightly spooky, and instead, I found myself in a bright, airy room decorated largely in yellow. It was like someone who loved sunshine had chosen the curtains, throw rugs, and accent pillows.

"This used to be a hospital room?" I asked as I dropped my tote bag onto the twin bed, which had a yellow and white gingham quilt on it.

"Yes. For those of us who live here, blocks of rooms were renovated into apartments. For guests, the individual hospital rooms were simply redecorated."

Felipe bounded to the window that looked out over the old cemetery behind the Sanctuary and the rolling hills beyond. It was dark out, so I couldn't see anything, but maybe he could.

"It's great, Mori. Thank you. I'll feel safer being here tonight."

Mori called Felipe to her, and when she turned to leave, I followed. "Are you joining the poker game?" she asked. "I'm convinced Malcolm cheats, though I haven't figured out how."

"No. Damien wants me to work on my conjuring skills. I think sleep is just an abstract concept to him."

Mori laughed. "When he was growing up here, he was awake during the day for school, but he still stayed up half the night with all of us. At least, he did, until he turned cold and unfriendly. He's quickly gotten back into the habit of living in both the daytime and nighttime worlds."

I knew Damien's attitude had changed when he had gotten into a fight during high school, and he had unleashed a burst of paranormal power. Baxter had taught him to hide it, but he hadn't bothered to tell his son what had happened or what kind of power it was. If I were Damien, I would have been resentful, too.

"Maybe I can conjure myself a huge cup of strong coffee," I mused.

I wished Mori luck in the poker game when we reached the entryway. She and Felipe headed in the direction of the dining room while I went down the hallway toward Damien's office. I hadn't reached it yet when he came out of the door, then turned and locked it.

I stopped short. "I thought we were going to practice tonight?" I really hoped he would say he'd changed his mind.

"We are."

Darn.

"Then why are you locking up? Do you want to go back to the mine again?"

"No. It's a nice night out, so I thought we'd practice outside." Damien walked past me and led me through several rooms until we eventually walked out a back door. I was familiar with the space since I had attended a Friday the Thirteenth party out there a few weeks before. There were picnic tables and a grill on a wide lawn.

I climbed up onto one of the picnic tables and sat on it, with my feet on the bench, and leaned back so I could look up at the sky. I could see so many more stars in Nightmare than I ever could in Nashville. It was a clear night, and the moon was bright enough for me to see Damien easily. There was just the hint of a chill in the air.

"What would you like me to do?" I asked. I turned my head toward Damien, who was pacing back and forth.

"When we were at the motel, I mentioned how important it is to be very specific in what you want to conjure. You had been focused on Lucy going home, but you should have been focused on us being alone." Damien paused, and I was on the verge of prompting him when he continued, "What specific thing could help you find out who killed Leonard? What detail would you most like to know?"

"Whether or not Sammy Simms stole from Leonard." I said it with zero hesitation. If I could prove the jewelry Tanner and McCrory had found in the plumber's office was the same jewelry Leonard had claimed was stolen from him, it would be enormously helpful. If the evidence was concrete enough, the police might even be able to use the information in their investigation.

"There you go." Damien paused his pacing long enough to look at me. "That's what you should focus on. Every ounce of your desire right now should be on finding out if Sammy stole from Leonard."

"I'll do my best." I shut my eyes and thought, *I want to know if Sammy stole from Leonard*, over and over.

I wasn't sure how long I sat there in deep concentration, but it was long enough that my arms were breaking out in goosebumps because I was getting cold. Even though it was still warm during the day, nights were becoming cool and crisp. Despite my discomfort, I continued to repeat that phrase again and again.

A voice suddenly spoke in a loud greeting. "I heard you two were out here." It was Vivian. I opened my eyes and turned to see her walking toward us. "Olivia, I remembered one more detail from my talk with Leonard that I thought you might be interested in. He said, and I quote,

'Alana told me my life was in danger, but my valuables were safe. Shows what she knows. That crook plumber took them.' I don't know if that helps."

Damien and I looked at each other and burst out laughing.

CHAPTER TWENTY-TWO

Vivian looked from Damien to me in confusion. "Why is that funny?"

"Damien brought me out here for some late-night conjuring practice," I explained. "I've been focused on my desire to know if Sammy Simms, the plumber, really did steal from Leonard. Then you showed up and mentioned Leonard's valuables."

"It's not perfect," Damien noted. "You didn't get the definitive answer you were looking for, but it shows your ability is growing, Olivia. Well done."

"Did Leonard say anything else about his valuables?" I asked Vivian.

"No. He mentioned them, then went right back to ranting about Alana's so-called psychic skills and wanting to know about his death."

"I appreciate the help, Vivian. I really think Sammy stole from Leonard, even if I can't prove it for certain. The question is, did he kill Leonard, too?"

"Keep focusing, and you'll find out soon enough!" Vivian wished us a good night and went back inside.

Once she was gone, I looked at Damien. "Wow," I said.

"Yeah. Good job, Olivia. I know you've been doing all this practice even while thinking it was pointless, but it's paying off."

I turned my face toward the sky again. Had Vivian's arrival and news been just another coincidence? Or had I really conjured magic that triggered her memory?

I was still having a tough time believing I was anything but normal.

When Damien spoke again, I could tell he was standing near me. He had finally stopped his pacing. "Let's call it a night," he suggested.

I straightened up and climbed down from the picnic table. I was cold, my lower back was starting to ache, and I was exhausted. There was no need to tell Damien I agreed with heading back inside, because he could probably see it in the way I trudged toward the door.

"Good night, Damien," I called when we reached the entryway. He was on his way to his office already, and I turned and went up the stairs.

When I was back in my room for the night, I washed my face in the chipped pedestal sink in the small bathroom, changed into my pajamas, and got into bed. The mattress wasn't the most luxe thing I had ever slept on, but it felt good just to be horizontal after such a long day.

The idea of spending the night at the Sanctuary had seemed comforting. The expectation and the reality of sleeping there turned out to be two very different things. No sooner had I turned out the light than I began wondering how many hospital patients had died in that very room. Then, I wondered if the room was haunted. Before I had come to Nightmare, I hadn't believed in ghosts. Tanner and McCrory had changed that.

As I lay there looking around the dark room, I heard a distant, high-pitched wail and shot bolt upright. My chest heaved as adrenaline coursed through me. "It's just Fiona," I told myself. "She probably lost a poker game, and she's wailing about it."

It made total sense that a banshee would wail when she lost at poker, right?

Eventually, I turned the light back on. I hadn't brought a book with me, but there was an old-fashioned wooden radio sitting on the nightstand. I turned it on, found a pop station, and finally drifted off to a ballad by the latest boy band.

It was the sound of breathing that woke me up the next morning. Deep, rhythmic noises that were definitely not coming from my own lungs sounded from somewhere near me. I cautiously cracked one eye open and was surprised to see sunlight glowing behind the yellow curtains. My gaze traveled down the bed, and I saw Felipe curled up at my feet, asleep.

How did he even get in here?

I sat up, stretched, and checked the time on my watch. It was nearly noon already. The shower in my room was cramped, so I did my best, then got dressed and wandered down to the dining room. Felipe was still fast asleep when I left.

Zach was just coming out of the dining room as I approached it. "Good morning," he said gruffly. "There's coffee if you want it." He jerked a thumb over his shoulder.

"Thank goodness supernatural creatures need coffee, too," I mumbled.

I found the big silver coffee machine not in the dining room itself, but in a large kitchen off of it. I had never been in there before, and it looked like a time capsule from the nineteen fifties. There were two squat white fridges and a stovetop that looked as big as my entire kitchen.

I found Morgan and Maida seated at a round table in one corner of the kitchen while Madge stood over a frying pan at the stove.

"I knew you were coming," Madge said in greeting, "so I added extra eggs."

"Thank you," I said as I found a coffee mug and poured a cup. "And good morning, ladies."

"You weren't murdered last night," Morgan said happily, the wrinkles around her eyes crinkling as she smiled.

"We're glad you're not dead," Maida added.

Sitting down to breakfast with three witches wasn't something I had ever pictured myself doing, but it felt remarkably normal. While we ate, we chatted about the cooling weather, and they filled me in on what to expect when the October crowds really started to ramp up.

I helped wash dishes once we finished breakfast. There didn't seem to be any reason to stick around after that, so I went back to my room to grab my tote bag. Felipe had disappeared, which was a mystery since I had shut my door when I went downstairs. Either chupacabras could open doors, or there was a hidden entrance to the room.

Not a lot of Sanctuary residents were awake at that hour, so I made my way down the staircase as quietly as I could. But, on a whim, I stopped in Damien's office before leaving. If he was already up and working, then I felt like I should check in with him.

Not only was Damien there, but I was amazed to see him dressed in jeans and a forest-green T-shirt that looked great against his lightly tanned skin. He rarely dressed so casually, which meant I rarely got a peek at his impressive biceps.

"Good morning, er, afternoon," I called to him. "I'm heading back to my apartment."

Damien looked up from the laptop on his desk. "By yourself?"

"Sure. It's daytime, and I'm awake, so I don't have to worry about being murdered in my sleep."

"I don't think you should be alone. I'll go with you."

"That's really not necessary."

"I'm going with you," Damien said firmly. He shut the laptop and stuffed it into a briefcase.

I hadn't had nearly enough coffee to be argumentative, so I drove home with Damien right behind me. He insisted on being the first one through my front door, too. He cracked the door, poked his head inside, then pushed the door wide. "It's safe."

"Now it's my turn to say I told you so," I said as I went in. I dropped my tote bag onto the kitchen table and looked around, wondering if Damien really did plan to stay all day. I was just opening my mouth to tell him he should go when I saw that one of my dresser drawers was halfway open.

Did I leave it like that last night in my hurry to pack?

I thought back. No, I hadn't even opened that drawer during my quick bag-stuffing session. I pointed to it. "It wasn't like that before."

"You think someone broke in here last night?"

I walked to the front door and yanked it open before carefully inspecting the lock and the edge of the doorframe for any sign someone had broken in. There was nothing.

"Sammy Simms got in here once," I said. "He didn't need to break in to do it." I reached out and caught the edge of the doorframe because I suddenly felt lightheaded. "I think Alana might have been right. Maybe Sammy came to kill me!"

"We don't know that," Damien cautioned, "but it does look like someone was going through your things."

"You're right: we don't know that for sure. Mama can scroll through the security cams, though. I know what his truck looks like."

Damien took me by the elbow. "Then let's get up there, right now."

I shook off his hand. "Not yet. Let me check and make sure nothing is missing." I doubted I had been robbed, though. Back in Nashville, I had owned a lot of things someone might want to steal. The one thing I still owned that was valuable was my purse, and that had been with me at the Sanctuary.

It didn't take long for me to confirm that my things were still right where they were supposed to be, so we headed for the front office.

Mama had a satisfied smile on her face the second she realized it was both Damien and me coming through the front door, but it immediately disappeared when I told her I thought someone had broken into my apartment. She agreed to check the video cameras and sat down to pull up the footage from the night before.

As Mama fast-forwarded through the video, she cleared her throat and said, "Damien, it's good to see you again."

There was a pause that was probably much shorter than it felt, then Damien said, "It's always good to see you, too, Mama." He shifted from one foot to the other and stared down at his T-shirt. "Am I supposed to call you Aunt Sue now?"

"Mama is just fine." Mama had her eyes fixed on the computer screen, but I could see her relax ever so slightly.

"There's the usual in and out until about ten o'clock," Mama announced eventually. "Then, there's not a single car on the footage until around seven-thirty this morning."

"It's a shame there aren't cameras trained on the rooms," I said.

Mama tapped a fingernail against the computer screen. "Who expects criminals to arrive on foot? We never saw a reason to have cameras anywhere else."

I thanked Mama and turned to go, then stopped as a sudden idea struck me. "Hey, can I work up here today? If someone was in my apartment, that might be the safer option." I gave Damien a pointed look.

Thankfully, Mama agreed, and Damien no longer had an excuse to stick around. In short order, I was settled in a lobby chair with my laptop. It wasn't until I'd been working for an hour that I said, "Whatever happened with Brian Wilcox's water pressure issue? Did Sammy come fix it?" I hadn't told Mama that I thought it was Sammy who had broken into my apartment.

"No, I had another plumber come take care of it. Between Sammy showing up in your room and Leonard accusing him of stealing, it felt like a good time to try out someone else."

Good woman, I thought.

I fell silent again, but there was something else on my mind, too. I got up and walked to the counter so I could look at Mama as she sat at her desk. "It's genetic, isn't it? You get vibes from people, and your sister was psychic."

"Yes. And I don't know what I'm going to say when Nick realizes his daughter is a psychic medium."

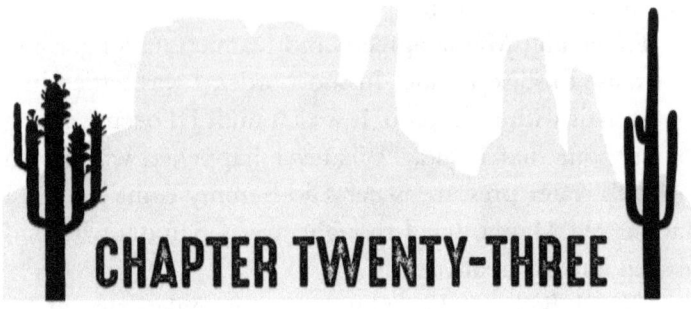

CHAPTER TWENTY-THREE

"A psychic medium?" I repeated. "I know Lucy has seen the ghost of a girl on the school playground, but she seems to think it's a real girl. The only reason I realized the truth is because Lucy talked about how the girl would be there one second and gone the next."

"Lucy has had other experiences, too," Mama said.

I smacked my forehead. "Like seeing her mother's spirit. She told me about the time Mia got electrocuted."

"Exactly. Lucy doesn't know how abnormal her experiences are, because she's so young. As she grows up, she's going to realize how different she is."

"I'm still trying to wrap my head around the fact that you know about the supernatural world."

Mama chuckled. "I about died laughing when I saw you walking a chupacabra one morning. What in the world were you thinking?"

I shrugged, as if taking Felipe for a walk hadn't been one of the more bizarre experiences of my life. "He had to go." I propped my elbows on the counter and narrowed my eyes at Mama, but I knew she could tell I was being playful. "At least now I know why you're always so excited when I spend time with Damien. I couldn't understand why you were so anxious for me to be nice to him, and it makes a lot more sense now that I know you're his aunt!"

"I couldn't tell him, but I still wanted the kid to be happy. Well, he's not a kid anymore. He turned into a very handsome man."

Mama looked at me expectantly, and I said grudgingly, "Yes, he's very handsome." Once I had admitted that to her, I returned to my chair so I could continue working.

Everything was quiet for a while, then the door opened, and I looked up to see Gabe and June walking through it. Gabe was, again, looking disheveled and haggard. If I'd had to guess, I would have said he was horribly hungover, even worse than when he had slammed the door on me. June looked tired but nowhere near as bad as her husband.

Gabe shuffled up to the counter in a graying white T-shirt and the same plaid pajama pants I had seen him wearing before. He didn't notice me, but June did, and she gave me a hesitant wave.

"It's our last night in town," Gabe said to Mama. "We want to make it memorable. What's the nicest restaurant around here?"

"What do you like?" Mama asked. "And how fancy do you want to go?"

"Top of the line." Gabe's lips turned up in a small smile, even while Mama gave him a look that said she didn't think he had the wardrobe to pull off dining at the nicest restaurant in Nightmare.

"There's a steakhouse in what's called the new downtown. It's where the city center moved to after the copper mine went bust, so despite the 'new' name, it's been downtown for around a century. I can call and try to get you a table, but it's a Friday night."

June hadn't seemed to be paying attention, but she gave Mama a skeptical look. "How can a town as small as this fill up a restaurant?"

Gabe ignored June. "We would appreciate it," he told Mama. "I could sure use a ribeye. Might help my head."

Oh, yeah, he's hungover.

Mama picked up the phone, and in short order, she was chatting with someone on the other end. Once she had made a reservation for eight o'clock and hung up, she told Gabe, "You're lucky. They just had a cancellation."

"Appreciate it," Gabe said, already turning to leave. That's when he finally spotted me, and he raised his hands to his face and mimicked fear just like he had at the Sanctuary. "Look, it's that spooky lady! Don't haunt me!"

I didn't bother to respond.

The second the door shut behind Gabe and June, I rocketed out of my chair and over to Mama. "You said they didn't give you killer vibes," I said, "but there is something off about those two. About Gabe, at least."

"I don't think either one of them is a murderer, but I do think they're obnoxious. And"—Mama leaned toward me and lowered her voice, even though we were alone—"rumor has it they're not completely honest, just like I said when you first asked me about them."

"Oh?"

"Apparently, he's been at the saloon every night, chatting people up and trying to get them to invest in some kind of real estate venture."

Real estate, just like Leonard and Brian were interested in. I was already forming a conspiracy theory, but Mama burst my bubble. "Of course, there is no real estate project."

"He's a con artist," I speculated.

"That's the rumor. He's getting people drunk, then convincing them to invest. And all they have to do is fork over a small down payment in cash."

I gaped at Mama. "That has to be illegal!"

"Seems like it should be. I'm guessing that by the time

the police find out, Gabe and June have moved on to the next little town. I'm sure it's no coincidence that the day they're the hot gossip is the same day they decide to leave Nightmare."

"And I'm guessing he'll be paying cash for that nice steak dinner."

The news that Gabe was conning people didn't take him off my suspect list. If he was willing to cheat people out of their money, then maybe he would be willing to kill, too. Maybe Leonard had refused to fork over any cash, especially after having his family jewelry stolen, and Gabe had killed him for it.

Then again, Mama hadn't gotten the feeling Gabe was responsible for Leonard's death, and I trusted her instincts.

"Are you going to teach her?" I asked suddenly. "Lucy, I mean."

"If she wants me to. She deserves a choice. My psychic abilities started to manifest when I was about her age, but I pushed them down. Lucille, obviously, fully embraced her gift."

"Did you ignore your ability because you were afraid of it?"

Mama looked wistful. "No. I wasn't afraid, and I didn't ignore it. I worked hard to keep it from becoming a part of me, because I just wanted to be normal. I was a self-conscious preteen who wanted to fit in with the cool kids."

"Speaking of the cool kids," I said gently, "when I was new here, and I told you I had a job interview at the Sanctuary, you sort of warned me about the people there being weird. Did you say that because you didn't want me to find out about the supernatural world?"

"I wasn't wrong! There are some real characters at that place." Mama chuckled, but then she dropped her eyes, and her shoulders sagged. "I've avoided the Sanctuary and those people since we lost Lucille. In that time, I've fallen into thinking of them the way the rest of this town does. It's wrong of me. Now that Damien knows the truth, I should rekindle some of my old acquaintances there."

"Do you really not know how your sister died?"

"Like I told you before, I'm not even sure she died. It's like she just—" Mama brought the fingertips of both hands together, then separated them quickly to mime an explosion. "She ceased to exist, at least in physical form, but I think her presence is still with us. I had a dream one night a couple months ago, and in it, I heard her voice. She told me to welcome the stranger. I woke up with no idea what it meant, but the next night, you came walking through the front door here, and I knew Lucille had meant you."

"No wonder you were so nice to me," I said. I felt flattered, but I also wondered how Mama's not-dead-but-not-living sister had known I would be arriving in Nightmare. At the time Mama had the dream, I hadn't even known the town existed, let alone that I would break down just outside it.

"That's not the only reason I was nice to you. I definitely got good vibes from you."

"Even as sweaty, tired, and broke as I was?" I laughed, then gasped. "Damien has always insisted I have a magical connection to Baxter, but what if my connection is with Lucille?"

CHAPTER TWENTY-FOUR

"Maybe Lucille is trying to help us find Baxter!" I said excitedly. "The job listing I found on the bulletin board at the Chamber of Commerce was in Baxter's handwriting, according to Damien. Then, I heard Baxter's voice coming from the mine, saying a phrase that he used to use."

Mama stared at me, her mouth hanging open. After a few attempts at saying something, she finally said, "You have so many things to fill me in on. I had no idea about any of this."

"I'll be happy to give you all the details, preferably over a beer at the saloon." I flashed Mama a smile, then quickly got serious again. "Damien thought these things meant Baxter and I had a connection, but what if Lucille orchestrated all of it? Damien wouldn't have recognized her handwriting or her voice, so maybe she's been acting like Baxter to get our attention."

"Maybe," Mama said slowly. She stared at a spot behind me as she thought. "If Lucille could visit me in a dream, then it's possible she could be doing other things, as well. Her body might have disappeared, but some part of her is still here."

"Maybe Vivian could communicate with her," I suggested. "She's a psychic medium."

Mama chewed her lip, mulling over the idea. After a

few moments, she nodded her head resolutely. "If she does, then I want to be there for it."

I grinned. "Great. This is exciting!"

It was impossible to get work done after that. Eventually, I gave up even trying. I wanted Tanner and McCrory to get another peek at Sammy Simms's office, so I scarfed down a quick lunch in my apartment, then headed for the Sanctuary.

Soon, I was driving toward Sammy's office, once again with Tanner and McCrory's shimmering forms in the back seat. Zach was sitting in the passenger seat, holding the wooden six-shooter box and giving me wary sidelong glances. Damien hadn't been around when I had arrived at the Sanctuary, but Zach had been there to let me into his office. When I told him why I needed to take the ghosts out for a bit, he had insisted on coming along. Considering Sammy might have tried to murder me the night before, it seemed like a good idea to have a werewolf as my backup, so I had welcomed Zach's company.

When I pulled up in front of Sammy's office, I was happy to see his truck was parked out front. If I could get myself inside his office, and if the jewelry was still there, then I could go to the police station with the tip.

Zach trailed behind me as I hurried to the door. Tanner and McCrory planned to circle around to the back of the building so they could look around while Sammy's attention was on me. I pulled on the door and almost cheered I was so happy it was unlocked.

I had known from looking through the glass door on my previous visit that Sammy's office was cluttered, but standing in it was a whole different experience. Cardboard boxes full of plumbing supplies towered nearly to the ceiling, and about half of the bulbs in the overhead lighting were burned out. It gave the place a dark, cramped atmosphere. I felt slightly claustrophobic, and I wondered how Sammy could sit at his desk, looking so calm.

Actually, his calm expression turned guarded as soon as he saw me. "You again," he muttered.

I held up both hands. "I came to apologize," I said. It seemed like a good excuse for being there. "I know my first visit here made it seem like I distrusted you."

Sammy stood and crossed his arms. "Distrusted? I got the feeling you thought I had killed that man at the motel."

Wow, had I really been that transparent?

I didn't have to feign embarrassment. It was absolutely real. Behind me, I heard Zach make a noise that might have been a snicker. "I was trying to help Mama and Benny, and maybe I got a little carried away," I said. "I'm sorry."

I glanced away from Sammy's glowering face and spotted Tanner standing in one of the back corners. He made a motion with his hands, and I realized he wanted me to draw Sammy away from his desk. I turned and took a step toward a stack of boxes, thinking I would ask Sammy some inane question about them that would require him to come toward me.

Unfortunately, there was a box on the floor in front of the stack, and I didn't see it until it was too late. My foot hit it, and I lost my balance.

By sheer good luck, I avoided landing on the pile of boxes and setting off a chain reaction. I figured if one stack went down, it would hit another, and another, and they would all go down, like a line of dominoes. Instead, it was only me who went flying. I landed on the narrow strip of carpet between the stack of boxes and a filing cabinet.

"Olivia, are you okay?" Zach asked. If he had been laughing at me before, at least he wasn't now.

I groaned. "My knee is going to have a big bump on it, but I think I'll live."

A hand floated into my range of vision, and I instinctively grabbed it, even while realizing it wasn't Zach helping me up. It was Sammy, and he was wearing a gorgeous—and very expensive—watch.

He really could be the one Alana saw killing me, I thought wildly. I fought to keep my fear out of my voice as I thanked him for helping me up. Out of the corner of my eye, I saw Tanner and McCrory both behind Sammy's desk. If nothing else, my fall had gotten Sammy to move.

I did a quick check to make sure my knee was the only casualty, then I both thanked Sammy and said goodbye to him all in the same breath. I was feeling even more embarrassed, and the ghosts had floated through the back wall, which meant their search was done.

The first thing I said when we were back in the car was, "Zach, if you tell anyone that I fell flat on my face—"

"You'll what? Conjure me into oblivion?" Zach laughed, and I swear, there was just the hint of a howl in his voice. Once he stopped laughing, he threw me a serious look. "I won't tell anyone. Promise."

"Thanks. Tanner, McCrory, what did you find?" I asked, looking at them in the rearview mirror.

"Not a thing," McCrory grumbled. "If he still has all that jewelry, then it's hidden."

"Makes sense," I said. I was disappointed, but I had, at least, learned that Sammy wore an expensive watch. Then again, so did Gabe. The way Brian dressed, I was sure he had a classy watch, too. Sammy's own choice in watches wasn't confirmation of anything.

I dropped off Zach and the ghosts at the Sanctuary, then headed home to get ready for work. I had just parked and climbed out of my car when I saw Brian walking in my direction.

"I hear Mama asked a different plumber to take care of your problem," I called. There was still a part of me that suspected Brian hadn't had low water pressure at all, and that his claim about it had just been an excuse to meet up with Sammy. I didn't know what their connection was, but I was convinced there had to be one.

Brian jumped when I talked to him, and he altered his course slightly so he wouldn't pass as closely to me, but he forced a smile onto his face. "Yeah, that plumber was great. He got my sink fixed in no time, and he told me where to find good barbecue in this town."

"Oh! That's nice to hear." I was stumbling over my words. Brian didn't seem like he was lying. Maybe he really was just a regular motel guest who'd had a regular plumbing issue. And, for some reason, I seemed to make him nervous. "I'm glad it worked out."

I gave Brian a little wave and headed for my apartment, feeling embarrassed yet again.

I left for work early that night, hoping to catch Damien beforehand. I wanted to tell him what Mama had said about his mother, and I wanted to present my suggestion that we ask Vivian to try communicating with her. When I got near Damien's office, though, I could hear him speaking in angry tones to someone. I caught something about "sneaking in" and "trespassing." It sounded like a local teenager had tried to get into the old hospital building. It happened from time to time, and it was one of the reasons Zach patrolled the grounds regularly.

I didn't wait to hear more of Damien's lecture. Instead, I headed to the dining room to wait for the family meeting. Justine was already there, so I filled her in on the latest developments—or, really, the total lack of them—in the murder investigation.

Once again, I was posted in the lagoon vignette that night. We had only been open for about an hour when Theo came up to me. There was a steady stream of guests coming through, so he looked menacingly at everyone walking past as he said, "Olivia, what— *You! Do you want to walk the plank? Then get out of here!* Sorry. You seem even more anxious than usual tonight, so I was— *I'll throw every one of you in the brig!* I was wondering if you're okay?"

"I'm looking at every wrist that goes past, in case the person attached to it likes expensive watches."

"This whole town knows that psychic is a fraud. No one is going to murder you."

"Let's hope." A group of giggling teenage girls was coming in my direction, and I lunged toward them. "What are you staring at?" I asked in a croaking voice. The girls squealed and screamed, and they dashed past me with their arms tightly around each other.

After that, I was more relaxed. Alana's prediction couldn't come true while I was working, and maybe Theo had a point. The rest of the night flew by, thanks to the unending stream of guests and the amount of fun I was having. I decided I even felt safe enough sleeping in my own bed that night. I purposely slipped out after work without stopping to talk to Damien, because I knew he'd try to convince me to sleep at the Sanctuary again.

By the time I got home, I was laughing at myself. Of course I wasn't going to be murdered in my bed. And, I told myself, I had probably left that dresser drawer open, and I had merely forgotten I had pawed through it for something.

I changed into my pajamas, washed my face, and realized that, prediction or not, I was ready for a good night's sleep. I pulled back the comforter and already had one foot off the ground so I could crawl into bed when I realized there was something wrong.

I put my foot down and stared at my bed, my heart feeling like it was in my throat. My sheets had been slashed.

CHAPTER TWENTY-FIVE

Someone *had* been in my room the night I had stayed at the Sanctuary. That meant I hadn't been the one who left my dresser drawer open. The intruder might have slashed up my bedsheets during that visit, or maybe they had come back a second time. Between me working in the front office of the motel, my visit to Sammy's office, and work at the Sanctuary, there were a lot of times someone could have snuck in. And, in a town as small as Nightmare, it would have been easy enough for someone to know that I worked at night.

Whenever it had happened was irrelevant. What mattered was that someone had broken into my apartment, and they had left me a warning.

My cell phone was on the nightstand, and I snatched it up. I probably should have called the police, but I called Damien, instead. "What?" he answered curtly. I didn't know what had been happening in his office earlier, but he was definitely in a bad mood.

"Someone was in my apartment." My voice sounded so small and childlike to my ears.

"Are you sure?"

"Yes. They slashed up my sheets. It's like Alana's prediction came true, but I wasn't here to be a part of it."

"Call the police. I'll be there in ten minutes." Damien

hung up, and I just stood there with the phone to my ear, still staring at the sheets. I felt dizzy, like the room was beginning to slowly rotate around me.

I drew in a long, slow breath, then dialed nine-one-one.

Not only did Damien beat the police to my apartment, but he did it in well under the ten minutes he had promised. No sooner had I hung up with the dispatcher than there was a knock on my door. I jumped and wondered what I had that could be used for self-defense, but then I heard Damien's voice calling my name.

I opened the door with shaking hands and pulled him inside, then slammed the door shut and re-engaged the security chain. "Look," I said, pointing toward my bed.

Damien did as instructed, but he quickly looked away. "That could have been you," he said quietly.

I nodded and was about to speak when there was another knock on the door. And, once again, I jumped. This time, though, I let out a shrill shriek, too.

"Nightmare Police," my visitor shouted. "Ms. Kendrick, it's me. Luis Reyes."

I let out my breath and opened the door to see Officer Reyes standing on my stoop, looking concerned. "Are you hurt?" he asked, giving me a quick once-over with his eyes. I was suddenly very cognizant of the fact I was wearing pajama shorts and a cropped T-shirt.

"I'm fine. I wasn't here when it happened."

Instead of relaxing, Reyes got a look on his face that parents give their children sometimes. "What have you gotten yourself into now?" He looked at Damien. "You've got your hands full with this one."

I started to protest that Damien did not have his hands full with me, but Damien beat me to the punch. "She's one of my employees at the Sanctuary. She's no more trouble than the rest of my team." There was something in Damien's voice, like he was daring Reyes to make a snide comment about the people who worked at the Sanctuary.

Luckily, Reyes didn't take the bait. He returned his attention to me and said, "Show me the damage."

I complied, and in the meantime, another two officers showed up. I didn't think I needed that many police officers on the scene for some slashed sheets, though their presence made me feel safer, at least. They went through my apartment thoroughly, but they found no other signs of the intruder. Just like when I had found the dresser drawer open, there wasn't any evidence of tampering with the lock on my door.

"Sammy Simms might have a skeleton key for the motel," I told Reyes. When he asked for clarification, I told him about Sammy's unexpected appearance in my apartment one morning and Mama's speculation that maybe he had gotten himself a skeleton key at some point during his years of doing plumbing jobs for the motel.

"You think Sammy broke in here to do this?" Reyes was looking at me like I was talking nonsense.

"Leonard accused Sammy of stealing his family jewelry, and I think he might be the killer," I retorted. My head was starting to hurt, and all I wanted was to go to bed with sheets that were crisp and whole.

Reyes shook his head, and the hint of a smile appeared. "Sammy didn't kill anyone. We had a long talk with him after you mentioned the stolen valuables, and he's got two alibis for that night. He and his wife were up with their sick son until dawn."

"Maybe they're covering for him," I said.

"You think a two-year-old is covering up a crime?" Reyes asked incredulously.

"No, but little kids don't count as alibis, do they?"

"His wife counts, and so does their family doctor. Sammy put in a call to him at one o'clock in the morning

171

to ask for advice on bringing down his son's fever. Ms. Kendrick, there is obviously someone who wants to warn you or hurt you, but it's not Sammy."

Who, then? I wondered. *Gabe? He knows I work at the Sanctuary, so maybe he snuck in while I was at work.*

I huffed out my breath. That theory didn't work, because Gabe wouldn't have had a key to my apartment. Only Sammy fit the bill, but if he hadn't killed Leonard, then he had no reason to come after me.

The police wrapped up in a couple of hours, and Reyes left with a promise to call me if they learned anything helpful. As soon as the police were gone, I headed to my bed and ripped off the comforter and sheets. I balled the sheets up, opened my front door, and dumped them unceremoniously on my front stoop. I would take them to the dumpster later. For the moment, I just wanted them out of my sight.

I was fishing another set of sheets out of my closet when I felt Damien's hand on my shoulder. "Olivia," he said.

"What?" I kept rummaging in the closet.

"You're not staying here, so there's no point in remaking your bed."

I turned around and looked at Damien pleadingly. "I shouldn't have to feel unsafe in my own home," I whined. "This isn't fair."

"I think you're right: if we find Leonard's killer, then we've found your intruder. You'll be perfectly safe as soon as the police wrap up the case. Pack a bag, and we'll head back to the Sanctuary."

"Okay." I couldn't keep the note of utter defeat out of my voice. I dutifully packed my tote bag again, double-checked that my dresser drawers were all closed this time, and we left.

Damien insisted on walking me up to the same guest

room I had slept in the night before, like he was afraid someone might attack me in the short walk from the entryway to the room. He even came inside and looked around, and I assumed he was making sure there wasn't a murderer hiding under my bed. Finally, he mumbled, "Good night" and left.

I slept terribly.

By the time I woke up on Saturday morning, my headache was still going strong, and my shoulder muscles ached from being so tense and scared. I took as hot of a shower as I could stand, then quickly put on shorts and a tank top so I could get to the coffee sooner rather than later.

As I was coming down the grand staircase, I saw Malcolm, Justine, and Damien standing there. Damien was gesturing with his hands, mimicking someone holding a knife, which meant he was filling the other two in on my adventure.

"Morning," I said. I didn't add the "good" because it wasn't a good morning.

"There she is," Malcolm said. "You look awful."

"Thanks."

"Come on," Justine said. "We're taking you to breakfast. You need about four cups of coffee and some bacon." She glanced at Damien. "You're welcome to join us." I could hear the hesitation in her tone. Damien always said no to offers like that, and no one really wanted him to be a part of their activities, anyway. Damien refusing every invitation seemed to make everyone happy.

I think we were all surprised, then, when Damien agreed to come with us. It was good for him, though. I had been encouraging him to go out and do things with people at the Sanctuary, or at the very least, to not be such a jerk to them. Maybe he was finally taking my advice.

Not only did Damien come with us, but he insisted on

driving, too, since I had left my car at the motel the night before. Malcolm barely fit in the front seat of Damien's Corvette, and Justine and I had our knees up under our chins in the back seat, but at least the drive to The Lusty Lunch Counter was a short one.

The Lusty was crowded when we arrived, and we snagged the last available booth. People stared at us as we settled in, and I really couldn't blame them. Justine and I looked pretty normal, but Damien was dressed in a suit, as usual, and he was wearing his mirrored sunglasses indoors. Malcolm was the one who really drew attention. He was always wearing his black top hat and long black coat, so even if he wasn't a vampire, he sure looked like one.

Ella was working behind the counter, and she gave me a wave. At least she wasn't judging our group.

I started to feel better once I had slurped down a cup of coffee. While we waited for our food, I told Justine and Malcolm my suspicions about Sammy breaking into my apartment, keeping my voice low enough that other diners wouldn't overhear. "I'm convinced the jewelry Tanner and McCrory saw under his desk was stolen from Leonard," I concluded. "I wish I could tip off the police, but I can't tell them the information came from a couple of ghosts."

Justine shrugged as she took a long sip of coffee. "There's no point telling them, anyway. That jewelry is long gone by now. I'm sure he pawned them."

I put down my coffee cup so I could drop my face into my hands. "Of course! I should have thought of that already! There has to be a pawn shop in Nightmare, right?"

My breakfast companions were so enthusiastic about helping me get some answers that they all volunteered to go with me, but I waved them off. "No, I think it might look odd if we all troop into the shop together."

"I'm going with you," Damien said firmly. "I'm not letting you out of my sight until this killer is caught."

It felt good to have a plan, and I ate my bacon and eggs quickly in my eagerness to get started. Luckily, my friends seemed to feel the same sense of urgency. Soon, Damien and I had dropped off Malcolm and Justine at the Sanctuary, and we were headed in the direction of the pawn shop.

I had pawned my fair share of things in the wake of my divorce, and the Nightmare pawn shop looked like every other one I had been in. I made a show of perusing the jewelry display, and when the owner came over and asked if I needed help, I said brightly, "Yes, thank you! I'm looking for some vintage jewelry. Preferably something with rubies."

"Vintage, huh?" The owner was a tall, heavyset man, and he scratched the back of his short brown hair while he thought. "I haven't had anything like that in a while. Probably not since old Betty Sanderson died, and her kids brought in the stuff they didn't want to keep."

I had been putting on an act, but when my face fell, it wasn't for show. "Okay," I said. "Thanks, anyway." *So much for that.*

"By the way," I added, "does Sammy Simms ever come in here to pawn stuff? I thought for some reason he had brought some old family jewelry here."

The owner frowned. "Sammy? The plumber? No, he never comes in here. His mother-in-law comes in from time to time, and it's always a wild assortment of stuff. Designer clothing, diamond earrings, and the most expensive watches you can imagine."

CHAPTER TWENTY-SIX

I raised an eyebrow at the pawn shop owner. "Expensive watches, huh?"

Damien had been silently standing next to me the whole time, and the man looked at him appreciatively. "I did notice you're wearing a nice piece yourself, sir. If you like, I can call you the next time I get something in."

"No, thank you," Damien said.

"Where does Sammy's mother-in-law get all these things?" I asked. If Sammy was stealing from people who hired him for plumbing jobs, it made sense he would have someone else pawn the items for him. It would be a perfect way to cover his tracks.

"She gets them through her work," the owner said. "Some of her clients pay her with whatever they have, then she brings the stuff in here."

It was like a little lightbulb suddenly turned on in my head. "Let me guess," I said, trying hard to keep my voice even. "People who don't have cash give Sammy's mother-in-law their valuables instead, because they're so desperate to know what their future holds."

The shop owner laughed. "Exactly! Even though most of this town knows she's just going to predict death for them. Gullible idiots. Still, it works out well for me."

I thanked him quickly, then I nearly dragged Damien

out the door. As soon as we were back in his Corvette, I said, "Sammy did steal from Leonard, and I'm guessing he's stolen from people he's worked for before. He gives the stolen goods to Alana, who can claim people gave them to her in exchange for a psychic reading."

"I agree that Alana is definitely laundering stolen goods for Sammy, but do you still think he killed Leonard?" Damien sounded uncertain.

"Yes. Remember what Leonard told Vivian about his conversation with Alana? Alana told Leonard he wasn't safe, but his valuables were. She must have known about the jewelry in his room, and she probably put Sammy up to finding it. Leonard's shower was probably never really broken. I bet Sammy weaseled his way in there, telling Mama he'd run into Leonard, who mentioned a bad shower, or something. It was Sammy's cover story to get into Leonard's room and find the jewelry. Later, when Leonard went back to Alana, he probably mentioned there was still some left that hadn't been stolen."

"So you think Sammy went back for the rest?"

"Why not? If he had a master key for the motel, it would have been so easy for him to slip in there while Leonard was out. Except he wasn't out, or he came back unexpectedly while Sammy was in the middle of robbing him, and they got in a fight that resulted in Leonard's death."

Damien braked at a stop sign, and he looked over at me while a semi rumbled past in front of us. "Was Leonard naked when you found him?"

I scrunched up my nose. "Ew, no! He had his clothes on. What kind of a question is that?"

"If the bathtub faucet was on when Leonard died, I thought maybe Sammy caught him mid-bath."

I choked out a noise that was part laughter, part disgust. "I didn't stick around to look at Leonard in detail, but I'm pretty sure he was in pants and a polo shirt." I caught myself chewing on a fingernail as I thought, and I clamped my hands together to keep myself from continuing to do it. It was an old nervous habit of mine, one that had been easy to keep in check by getting weekly manicures.

I glanced down at my hands. *I sure do miss having nice nails. I miss that emerald ring, too. I'd still have both of those things if Mark hadn't*— "Oh!" I suddenly said. "It's so obvious, isn't it? I bet Sammy showed up while Leonard was in the middle of stuffing the jewelry down the drain. He was trying to hide it, right as the person he wanted to hide it from showed up! He probably turned on the faucet to make it look like he was going to take a bath, so Sammy wouldn't guess the hiding place."

"It's a plausible guess," Damien said. We were moving again, and Damien was tapping the steering wheel as he thought.

"I think we should share what we've learned today with the police." I started to fish my phone out of my purse, but I stopped. "Just take me to the police station. I'll tell them in person."

"It's a long shot, Olivia," Damien warned me.

"I know, but I want to—" I broke off abruptly. We were driving right past Alana's home and business, and there was a Nightmare Police car parked outside. "They already know she's involved! Pull over!"

"Maybe we should let the police do their work."

"Damien, please!" We were already past Alana's by then. Damien glanced at me, made a noise of resignation, and made a U-turn.

Damien pulled into an empty parking spot in front of Alana's business, and I had the door open before the car had stopped moving. I was almost to the front door when I heard my name being called. I turned and saw Officer Reyes climbing out of the police car.

I grinned at Reyes. In hindsight, I probably looked a little unhinged. "You're here to get a confession, I see," I said excitedly.

Reyes squinted at me, "You okay, Ms. Kendrick? I'm here to get a reading."

My smile froze in place, and it seemed to take extra time for my brain to process what Reyes had just said. "What?" I asked.

"I get a reading from Alana every month. What would she be confessing to, anyway?"

"To being in cahoots with Sammy Simms, her son-in-law!" I didn't give Reyes a chance to disagree with me, and I didn't stop to laugh at myself for actually using the word *cahoots*. Instead, I laid out my whole theory to him, barely stopping to take a breath between words.

"You're not coming inside with me," Reyes said when I had finished.

"Please?"

Behind me, I heard a squeak, and I turned to see Alana opening her front door. "What's going on out here?" she asked nervously.

"Nothing," Reyes said quickly. He excelled at giving someone the hairy eyeball, and I crossed my arms but stayed silent under his gaze. "I'm just coming inside for my reading, Alana."

Reyes began to move past me, and I whispered to him, "She and Sammy have a racket going."

There was no way Alana could have heard me, but she took a step back and began to close the door. "We'll reschedule!"

"Alana, wait!" Reyes dashed toward the front door, but Alana had already slammed it shut. He rounded on me angrily. "See what you've done? You upset her!"

"I didn't say a word to her!"

Reyes shook his head and knocked on the door. "Alana, she won't bother you. Please open up."

If there was ever a time for me to use my conjuring skills, this was it. *Confess,* I thought. *Open the door, confess to Reyes, and tell him how Sammy was stealing from your clients. Give up every detail of your laundering racket. Confess, confess, confess.*

After Reyes knocked two more times, Alana slowly opened the door. "Go away."

"I'm so sorry Ms. Kendrick upset you, but I assure you, she's leaving." Reyes craned his neck around and glared at me.

Alana was looking at me, too, with something like hurt on her face. "I tried to help you," she wailed.

"By telling me you had foreseen my murder?" I asked. "In your vision, you said my killer was wearing an expensive watch. Was it like the ones you pawn?"

"It wasn't a vision. It was a warning!" Alana pushed her way past Reyes, and her grandmotherly demeanor transformed as she began to shout at me. "You were poking your nose into things you shouldn't, and when I told Sammy we needed to lay low, he said he would just get rid of you, instead. But I told him one murder was enough. In all our years doing this, we never hurt anyone, let alone—!"

Reyes looked stunned. "Are you telling me Sammy killed Mr. Evers?"

Alana clapped a hand over her mouth, realizing she had said too much, but I answered for her. "No. Sammy has an alibi for the night. Alana killed Leonard."

CHAPTER TWENTY-SEVEN

Alana shook her head wildly, then she lowered her hand a fraction. "One of the times Leonard came back here, he told me his valuables had been stolen, even though I had said they would be safe. Then he dropped the fact that he still had some left, so I went there to get the rest. I knew he would let me in if I promised to tell him more predictions for his future. I waited until late, when no one would see me, and I parked in the alley behind the motel."

"What happened at the motel, Alana?" Reyes asked.

"I knocked on Leonard's door and called his name for a long time, and eventually, he answered. He had the bathtub running. He told me to have a seat while he turned it off, but halfway to the bathroom, he turned and asked me flat-out if I was working with Sammy. He had figured out that I was the only one in Nightmare who knew about his jewelry and where he was keeping it, so Sammy didn't have to tear the place apart looking for it."

"So you killed him?" Reyes still looked completely shocked by Alana's confession.

"Of course. I didn't want Sammy to get into trouble." A tear ran down Alana's face, but she still had enough fire in her to give me an angry look. "When Sammy said he was going to kill you to keep you from finding the truth, I asked him not to. But he said he had to do it to protect both of us. So I gave you that warning in the hope you'd take precautions. You're not dead, so you obviously listened to me. I was trying to save your life, and now you've ruined mine."

I really didn't feel bad about that. According to what Fiona had told me, Alana had gone to Leonard's room that night intending to kill him. Leonard figuring out she was working with Sammy had probably only solidified her decision to quiet him forever.

Reyes handcuffed Alana and put her in the back of his car. Before he climbed into the driver's seat, he came over to me and extended his hand. As I shook it, he said, "Well done, Ms. Kendrick. We'll collect Sammy, too, so you don't have to worry about another attempt on your life."

Reyes pulled onto the road, churning up a huge cloud of dust, and I coughed. Damien stepped up next to me. "Wow," was all he said.

"Yeah. I think I might have just conjured her confession. I was focusing so hard on her giving up details of the laundering racket. Of course, she confessed to murder, instead, so it wasn't quite what I had been trying to conjure. I guess I need to keep practicing." I tried to laugh, but it came out like more of a high-pitched squeak.

"Well done, Olivia. We'll tell the others tonight. They'll be excited to know you found the killer and that you're safe."

"How about that?" I said as we returned to Damien's car. "Alana's prediction about a man with an expensive watch trying to kill me was true, after all."

"Except she didn't learn about it through her alleged psychic skills."

Instead of dropping me off in the back corner of the motel, where my apartment was, Damien parked right in front of the Cowboy's Corral office. We both went inside, and Benny wished us a hearty good morning. I looked at my watch, amazed. We had eaten breakfast, gotten a lead at the pawn shop, and caught the killer, and it wasn't even noon yet.

As Damien and I returned Benny's greeting, Mama came in the door behind us. "Good morning, you two." She gave me a little wink, and I wondered just what she thought Damien and I were doing together. "I brought cinnamon rolls."

Even though I had already eaten breakfast, I gladly grabbed a roll out of the box in Mama's hands. I took a giant bite while Damien said proudly, "Leonard's killer has just been arrested, thanks to Olivia."

Benny cheered while Mama said anxiously, "Who was it? What happened? Are you two okay?"

I swallowed even as I laughed. "Yes, we're fine. Everyone's favorite fake psychic killed Leonard."

"Alana?" Mama's eyes grew wide.

Damien and I explained everything while Mama and Benny gave us their full attention. And it really was their full attention. Brian Wilcox walked in while I was in the middle of telling them about the visit to the pawn shop, and Mama completely ignored him. When Brian said, "Excuse me," Mama held up her finger and told him to wait.

"Sorry," I told Brian apologetically. "It's just that Leonard's murder has been solved, and I'm filling them in."

Brian looked down and rubbed a hand against the back of his neck. "It wasn't you, then?" he asked me.

"Me?"

Mama and Benny both laughed at my obvious surprise.

"Some of the stuff you said to me was a little weird." Brian shrugged. "Plus, you were at the crime scene the morning after he died, and then you were there again when they found more evidence. I thought maybe you were the criminal who came back to enjoy their handiwork."

I felt my cheeks flush. "I thought the same thing about you. Since you were out here looking for real estate, like Leonard, and since you were both from Ohio, I thought you'd followed him here and killed him."

"Nope, those were just coincidences."

There was that word again.

"To be fair," I said in my defense, "you were acting strange at the crime scene. You were just staring into Leonard's room, and you called him an 'it.'"

Brian actually laughed. "I was acting strange because someone at the motel where I'm staying got killed! And, once I heard the rumor about the stolen jewelry, I got nervous. I've got a few nice things in my suitcase, and I didn't want to be the next victim."

"I'm sure you were safe," Mama noted. "I'm guessing Sammy only ever stole from Alana's clients. She would get them to tell her secrets, like what valuables they had and where they were kept, and the next time Sammy paid them a visit as their friendly neighborhood plumber, he would rob them. It explains why none of our motel guests ever got robbed when Sammy would come here to fix a plumbing issue. His victims weren't random."

"You're probably right," I told Mama, "though Sammy did go into Brian's room, remember? He claimed it was a regular plumbing check."

Brian glanced down and ran a hand lightly over his button-down shirt, which looked perfectly tailored. "I suppose I looked like I might have something worth taking."

I apologized to Brian for thinking he might be a killer, then Benny quickly got him checked out. On his way out the door, Brian looked at me mischievously. "Thanks for making my trip here so memorable. I'll look you up when I return to get my new property fixed up."

"The first round at the saloon is on me," I promised.

Damien and I finished our story once Brian left, and Mama and Benny both expressed relief to finally have the ordeal over with.

"And I'm hiring a locksmith next week to change the locks on every room," Mama said. "I don't know how Sammy got his hands on a skeleton key, but he's not going to get in your place or any other room again!"

"Especially while he's in jail. I know he won't be locked up forever, but I'll sleep better knowing he's not around for a while." I took another huge bite of cinnamon roll. Solving murders really worked up my appetite.

After I swallowed, I said, "Here's what I don't get. Sammy even told me how Leonard had ranted about the town psychic. Of course, he never mentioned Alana was his mother-in-law, but why would he say something that might make her look like a suspect? She's his family!"

"No honor among thieves," Benny said. "Or he said it without realizing it implied she might have been involved in the murder."

"I still can't believe they were secretly related," I said. I waved what remained of my cinnamon roll toward Mama. "Just like you and Damien!"

Damien shuffled his feet awkwardly at that comment, but Mama laughed. "Lots of folks know Sammy married Alana's girl. It was never a secret. You just didn't know because you're new in Nightmare."

I stared at my cinnamon roll like it had betrayed me. Maybe what I really needed was another cup of coffee. Of course Alana being Sammy's mother-in-law wasn't some big, scandalous secret.

"Speaking of being related, Damien," Mama said, "I've got something for you to see." She dropped the box of cinnamon rolls onto the counter, then walked around to her desk. She hefted a thick photo album with a brown leather cover and placed it on the counter next to the box. "Family photos."

Damien opened the cover, and on the first page, there was a photo of two young girls sitting on a couch. The sepia tones of the photo and the style of their clothing showed it was old. Mama pointed at the smaller girl. "That's me. The other one is your mother."

I looked over at Damien, uncertain how he was going to react.

He was smiling.

A NOTE FROM THE AUTHOR

Wow, y'all, some of the bombshells in this book caught even me by surprise! I'm enjoying exploring the characters and stories in the fictional town of Nightmare, and I'm grateful that you're along for the ride! Thank you for being a part of this fun adventure.

Before you go, will you please leave a review for *Murder at the Motel*? It really helps indie authors like me, and I appreciate your support.

Eternally Yours,

Beth

P.S. You can keep up with my latest book news, get fun freebies, and more by signing up for my newsletter at BethDolgner.com!

FIND OUT WHAT'S NEXT FOR OLIVIA AND THE RESIDENTS OF NIGHTMARE, ARIZONA!

Poisoning at the Party

NIGHTMARE, ARIZONA BOOK FIVE
PARANORMAL COZY MYSTERIES

Candy, Chaos, and Conjuring in Nightmare, Arizona

There's a new fairy in town, and no one in Nightmare, Arizona, is happy about it. Olivia Kendrick learns why when she and Annabelle team up to help out at the annual Nightmare Fall Festival.

When Annabelle is found dead inside the corn maze the night of the festival's kickoff party, the police don't think it's murder. Olivia and her supernatural friends at Nightmare Sanctuary Haunted House know better, and it will be up to them to catch the killer.

Even as Olivia closes in on the truth of Annabelle's murder, her boss Damien seems further away than ever. Can Olivia convince him to explore his own paranormal power so the two of them can find his missing father?

Coming March 2024. Pre-order now!

ACKNOWLEDGMENTS

It might be my name on the cover, but it takes a team of people to publish a book, and I'm so grateful for everyone involved. It begins with my test readers Sabrina, Lisa, Kristine, Mom, David, and Alex. My editors, Lia at Your Best Book Editor and Trish at Blossoming Pages, take it from there. When the manuscript is ready to go, Jena at BookMojo gets it formatted, designs a gorgeous cover, and helps me get it out there in the world. And, finally, thank you to my team of ARC readers—I am so grateful for each of you!

ABOUT THE AUTHOR

Beth Dolgner writes paranormal fiction and nonfiction. Her interest in things that go bump in the night really took off on a trip to Savannah, Georgia, so it's fitting that her first series—Betty Boo, Ghost Hunter—takes place in that spooky city. Beth also writes paranormal nonfiction, including her first book, *Georgia Spirits and Specters*, which is a collection of Georgia ghost stories.

Beth and her husband, Ed, live in Tucson, Arizona, with their three cats. They're close enough to Tombstone that Beth can easily visit its Wild West street and watch staged shootouts, all in the name of research for the Nightmare, Arizona series.

Beth also enjoys giving presentations on Victorian death and mourning traditions as well as Victorian Spiritualism. She has been a volunteer at an historic cemetery, a ghost tour guide, and a paranormal investigator.

Keep up with Beth and sign up for her newsletter at BethDolgner.com.

BOOKS BY BETH DOLGNER

The Nightmare, Arizona Series

Paranormal Cozy Mystery

Homicide at the Haunted House

Drowning at the Diner

Slaying at the Saloon

Murder at the Motel

Poisoning at the Party (March 2024)

The Betty Boo, Ghost Hunter Series

Romantic Urban Fantasy

Ghost of a Threat

Ghost of a Whisper

Ghost of a Memory

Ghost of a Hope

Manifest

Young Adult Steampunk

A Talent for Death

Young Adult Urban Fantasy

Nonfiction

Georgia Spirits and Specters

Everyday Voodoo

www.ingramcontent.com/pod-product-compliance
Lightning Source LLC
Chambersburg PA
CBHW020434180626
46812CB00003B/1230